To

Sadia,

Experience the magic
of Bollywood...

Best wishes,

Puneet

x

For forthcoming titles in the glamorous,
star-studded Bollywood Series, visit…

www.bollywoodseries.com

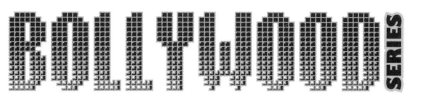

BOLLYWOOD SERIES

Starlet Rivalry

Puneet Bhandal

FAMOUS BOOKS

FAMOUS BOOKS

First published in 2009 by Famous Books
2 St Peters Rd, Southall, Middlesex UB1 2TL
Email: info@famousbooks.info

ISBN: 978-0-9560255-0-0

Printed in England

A CIP catalogue record for this book is available from the British Library.

www.famousbooks.info

For Bollywood fans everywhere

Chapter 1

Bela could just about make out Monica's voice in the corridor outside her dressing room.

'Well, she seems to have forgotten that *I* was here long before her. I made the headlines just by being born 'cos everyone knew my mum and dad. Bela's just an outsider who's got lucky, but she reckons she's the best. I'm telling you, she had better watch her tongue.'

'Yeah,' added a female voice that Bela couldn't quite place. 'Who does she think she is? You're a much better actress, Monica. Bela's only made a few films and she thinks she's so perfect. She acts like such a goody-goody, but she's really big-headed and a fake. I'm sure Marc would much rather work with you than her.'

Bela heard a lot of girlie giggling, and then the click-clack-click of high heels beating on the concrete floor as the girls walked off. The laughter was still audible but, thankfully, it was fading fast.

'A fake!' exclaimed Bela, pulling her chair back and looking up at the make-up artist who had overheard the conversation too. 'Really? Is that what people think of me? And do I come across as big-headed?'

Micky stepped forward and carried on touching up her eye-shadow. Bela was on a break during the filming of the romantic movie *My Love* in which she was starring opposite Bollywood's hottest heartthrob Marc Fernandez, and she only had a few more minutes before she needed to be back on the set.

Before Micky even had a chance to comment, though, Bela was off again. 'I've seen them huddled up in corners, having these secret conversations since yesterday. I sensed they were talking about me but then I thought maybe I was just being paranoid. I don't even know why Monica's hanging around here – she's not even in the film!'

Bela pondered for a while and then, when Micky stopped to get a different brush, walked over to the door to shut it so that nobody could eavesdrop. 'So it's true what they said on the *Bollywood Grapevine* website? Monica really doesn't like me, does she? But why not? I haven't done anything to her.'

Her head was spinning.

Micky, on the other hand, was privately quite amused by the accidental revelations. After twenty years in the business he was quite used to this sort of thing, but he tried to keep a straight face for Bela's sake. She was very young and he realised this must be a big deal for her right now. He had got to know her quite well over the last six months and found her to be anything but conceited.

'Yes, honey, I know it's terrible,' he said when Bela had calmed down a bit. 'But people also say that you don't like her much either. If there's no truth in that, perhaps it's fair to say there's no truth in the rumour that Monica hates you.'

'But I just heard her talking about me.'

'Okay she's gossiping here and there about you,'

acknowledged Micky, 'but you've got to realise that's how it is around here. This is Bollywood, my darling! Maybe she's reacting to something that she's seen or heard.'

Bela stopped to think while Micky continued working his magic. Even if he was right – that she was reacting to something – there was something about Monica that made Bela feel very uneasy. Monica happened to be the daughter of a very successful couple: her parents were actor-turned-film-maker Shashi Kumar, and popular heroine Malaika Rani. Monica was a true star-child.

It wasn't Monica's heritage that Bela resented, though. She'd grown up watching Shashi Kumar and Malaika Rani in the movies and she admired them. It was more the fact that Bela had heard from various sources that whenever Monica and another actress were signed up to co-star in a film, Monica was the one who got the most popular song sequences, the exotic locations and the best dialogue. Even more suspiciously, the films apparently never kept to the original scripts and the changes were always to Monica's advantage.

Micky was almost finished with Bela's make-up now. He dabbed powder on her brow and then paused. He picked up a bag that was lying nearby.

'I wasn't sure whether to show you this,' he said, removing from the big black holdall a creased-up copy of *FilmGlitz* magazine.

'This is what I meant when I said Monica may be reacting to something.' A cover line – in bright red capital letters – screamed, 'STAR WARS: BELA-MONICA FIGHT HOTS UP'.

'See that?' he said, pointing to the sensational words. 'If an outsider read it, they'd be sure you must hate her too.'

Bela's big brown eyes opened wide and she threw an anxious glance at Micky before snatching the magazine out of his hands. 'Oh my God!' she exclaimed, staring at the cover, which had a photo of Bela and Monica standing with their backs to each other and wearing rather stern expressions.

'What's this all about?' she questioned. 'I don't get it. I'm so careful not to say bad things about any of the other girls in my interviews or on set.'

'Well, can't argue with you there Bela. I've never heard you bad-mouth anyone.'

'So where does this kind of stuff come from? Have you read the story, Micky? What does it say?' Bela was extremely flustered, and hurriedly flicked through the pages in an attempt to find the offending article.

'Come on now, Bela,' urged Micky, snatching the magazine back from her and glancing at the wall clock. 'Don't get yourself all worked up. You'll be hot and sweaty in no time and I'll have to do you up all over again.'

'But Micky, I need to know what it says about me. Is it really awful?'

'Go finish your shoot and worry about it later. You don't want Marc to see you looking anything less than perfect, do you?'

'Ha ha, very funny,' Bela retorted, giving him a friendly shove. 'Don't go starting fresh rumours, I've got enough on my plate as it is. I'd better go,' she added quickly, suddenly aware that the crew would be waiting for her. 'Look at the time. Leave that magazine on my chair, please. I need to read it when I get back.'

As Bela made her way back towards the set, smoothing down her long brown hair with her hand, she tried to work out where the story about the alleged spat could have originated from.

She was feeling quite burdened now – by the gossip mills but also by the gorgeous green gown she was wearing. She had a slim, curvaceous frame and her dress was so heavily encrusted with glass beads that Bela felt she needed to sit down again just to take the weight off her feet. Luckily, there was an old wooden chair nearby.

'Hi there, Miss Bollywood,' came a voice from behind her. 'You're looking very glam in green.' It was Marc.

'Oh, hi Marc,' smiled Bela, pushing aside a few loose strands of hair that were falling on her face.

'I hear you've been dancing the socks off even the choreographer today,' he said. 'I can't wait to see the rushes.'

'Well, we'll see the final result and then find out what everyone thinks,' smiled Bela modestly as she got to her feet again. She didn't want to sit while Marc was standing so she stood nervously beside the hunky six-footer.

'How've you been?' she asked.

'Yeah, girl, I've been good. I've just got back from the gym. See these?' he asked, flexing his biceps. 'The result of much hard work, I can tell you. And we don't get paid extra for these heavy workouts, it's all part of the job now. Being a film star isn't just about acting any more, is it? Personally, I blame Stallone.'

'Yeah, you're probably right,' said Bela. 'It was different in the old days. Top actors might have had nice faces, but let's be honest, none of them had a body like *that*,' she added, nodding towards Marc's rippling torso.

'Well those guys never needed to strip off, did they?' said Marc. 'I mean, look at the love scene we're gonna be filming later. Why is it that I'll be wearing jeans and no top while you get to keep all your clothes on? Not fair, I say.'

Bela blushed ever so slightly and hoped that Marc didn't notice. She had such fair, translucent skin that even a small rush of blood to her face meant she went quite pink.

'Well, luckily for me, we're in Bollywood, not Hollywood, or I'd probably be topless too!' she joked.

The pair laughed out loud and at that moment Bela caught sight of Monica, looking extremely eye-catching in a summery white dress with yellow polka dots, bright yellow heels and sunglasses, walking on to the set with a pal. The two girls saw Bela and Marc and immediately started whispering to one another.

'Why are they laughing at us?' enquired the friend.

'Ignore them, so childish,' snapped Monica. 'Mind you, he's okay, it's her.' She turned around and directed her gaze at Bela. 'She must be telling Marc that's she's better than me – she can't help herself, obviously,' Monica added as they stepped through the door at the far end of the studio.

'Whoa! If looks could kill, you'd be dead, Bela,' said Marc, once Monica was safely out of sight.

'Oh dear, I bet she thinks we were laughing at her,' said Bela. 'I heard her talking earlier outside my make-up room. For some reason, Monica seems to think I don't like her and I'm pretty sure now that she hates me. I have no idea how it got like this, but it's so uncomfortable when we're in the same studio. What's she doing here, anyway? I just can't seem to get away from her.'

'Well,' replied Marc, bending down to zip up one of his metal-toed cowboy boots, 'she's probably thinking the same thing about you. This is her dad's studio, after all!'

'Is it really?' Bela looked surprised. 'I didn't know, but that explains why she's here. I'll try not to annoy her any further, even though it's pretty hard since I don't know what started all this in the first place.'

As Marc stood up again, Yogi, the director of *My Love*, suddenly rushed on to the set and started shouting orders at all the unit members to get a move on. Marc and Bela were ready, but she didn't really want to move.

Just talking to Marc about the Monica issue

made Bela feel better. It didn't seem like such a big deal now. Besides, she was glad to have something to talk to him about. Normally, she was a bit lost for words when he was around.

Bela felt Marc must know she had a huge crush on him, but it was probably no big deal for him because so did every other female in India. He had the most impossibly handsome face – his deep, dark eyes and well-defined jaw gave him a really smouldering look.

When his first movie was released Bela was a piggy-tailed schoolgirl of twelve, while Marc was seventeen. She'd plastered his posters over her bedroom walls and all the other girls at school had done the same. But things changed really quickly after she won a classical dance competition. She'd received a film offer immediately afterwards and now, at just sixteen, Bela was in the enviable position of being able to work with the man that millions of girls lusted after.

'My make-up man, Micky, was showing me the cover of *FilmGlitz* today,' continued Bela, ignoring the buzz of activity now going on around them. 'It had an article that says me and Monica are at war. How mad is that? We've hardly ever spoken to one another.'

'Yeah, I glanced over that at the gym,' said Marc. 'No wonder she's mad.'

Bela froze. 'What did it say?' she asked quietly, almost afraid to hear the reply.

'Oh, I didn't read it all. I try not to read that stuff,' Marc went on, leaning back against a pillar and folding his arms as though to emphasise his muscles. 'It's something about you saying that Monica may have the Bollywood breeding, but she's still a B-grade actress while you're now firmly on the A list.'

'What? That's terrible!' shrieked Bela.

A few people working nearby turned to look at her. She lowered her voice. 'I can't believe it! I have *never* said that about her.'

'Never?' asked Marc.

'Yes, never! I wouldn't say it about anyone. It's not up to me who's A or B list. I don't even think there is a list! Oh God, no wonder she hates me. I would, if I were in her shoes!'

Aware of her little outburst and concerned that Marc might be thinking she's a moaning minnie, Bela decided to stop ranting. Instead, she sat back down on the wooden chair and changed her tune.

'I actually admire the way she's transformed herself,' Bela remarked, looking up at Marc who was listening intently. 'You know she was at the same school as me, one year above?'

'Was she?' said Marc. 'I thought she was a few years older than you.'

'No, she's not much older, just a year or so. But if you had seen her when she was twelve or thirteen, you would never believe it's the same girl.'

'Yep,' he nodded. 'I've heard about her "ugly duckling" phase.'

'Hey, careful! I never used those words. I don't want that showing up in another magazine!'

'Trust me, it won't,' assured Marc.

'Good. Well, going back to what I was saying, Monica was a bit geeky-looking when she was twelve – she had braces, bad hair and was quite chubby,' described Bela. 'Then, one summer, she must have worked really hard on her looks 'cos the next thing we all knew was that she'd transformed herself into a real stunner and suddenly had all these modelling offers flooding in! We never saw her at school after that.'

'She's gorgeous, that's for sure,' agreed Marc. 'I actually reckon she's better suited to the modelling world than movies, but she decided otherwise and persuaded Papa dearest to make a film for her,' he added as he looked over to the set again to see if they would be ready to shoot any time soon.

'Oh look, time to head back, director *sahib's* gesturing at us. Don't worry about the magazines Bela – they're nothing but gossip rags. Just think about the next scene and you'll be fine.' He strode off in the direction of the set.

Bela smoothed down her dress and was adjusting her straps when Marc stopped, turned around to look at her again and whispered, 'And when you say you love me for the camera, look as though you mean it.'

She let out a small nervous laugh. Bela wasn't quite sure what he meant by that but there was no time to think about it right now. She put it to the back of her mind, making a note to try and decipher it once she got back home.

Bela followed Marc over to where Yogi was waiting and he gave the pair some quick instructions before positioning them before the camera. In accordance with the script, Marc removed his T-shirt and stood there in just his jeans and cowboy boots. Bela was suddenly very nervous again. She was so worried that she'd come across as a gushing teenager, swooning over this hot bare-chested hunk, that she was completely tongue-tied.

In this scene, the character Bela was portraying,

called Saaya, was upset because her rich father was trying to stop her from meeting her lover Vikram, played by Marc. Saaya had just slipped away from a family function where her dad was due to announce her engagement to someone called Ravi, so Bela had to look as though she was seriously distressed.

She cleared her throat and began: 'Vikram... I miss you so much. Papa is determined to keep us apart, but I don't want to live without you. And I can't marry anyone else. I want to be with you all the time. I can never belong to Ravi and I will never marry him. I... I... I... love you, Marc.'

'CUT!' Yogi yelled. 'Bela, Bela, Bela! My darling, whether you love Marc or not is your business, but for the purposes of this film, try to remember you need to call him Vikram.'

Everyone on the set roared with laughter. Bela turned a shade of crimson.

'Sorry,' she whispered, but the laughing carried on. Marc seemed to be the only one who wasn't joining in. 'Come on guys, it wasn't that funny,' he shouted out to his colleagues, in an effort to get them to stop.

It didn't help and to make matters worse, when Bela got the courage to look up again, she saw Monica and her chum standing a few feet behind the camera, laughing their heads off too. In fact, Monica was bent double, clutching her tummy as though it was so hilarious she couldn't stand up straight.

'The truth is out now!' she called. 'Marc, she loves you!'

'Aaah, come on, Monica,' he hollered back. 'How about we all just grow up a bit?'

Monica, none too pleased with that comment, straightened herself up, then linked arms with her pal and stalked off.

'Come on, Bela,' said Marc. 'It's no big deal, everyone makes mistakes. Let's have another go. I know you'll be fine this time. We need to get through this scene – there's a lot more to do today.'

He spoke loudly and professionally as if he was also trying to relay a message to the onlookers to stop the cackling and get on with the job.

Bela took a deep breath, recomposed herself and started again. Marc was right. This time there were no mistakes. She delivered her dialogue with the same emotion as before, then held Marc's hands in hers, gazed into his adorable eyes and with real intensity, whispered, 'I love you Vikram… I love you.'

'Cut!' shouted Yogi again. 'Wow! That was really

good, very believable. I think your screen chemistry is mind-blowing!'

Bela smiled, feeling proud, but also relieved that she had managed to remedy such a squirmingly embarrassing situation so quickly.

'Well done, Bela,' said Marc, approvingly. 'I knew you'd be fine. You're gonna be one of the *very* best, I know it.'

Bela thanked him for the compliment and then, hoisting her dress up ever so slightly to stop it from dragging along the dusty floor, began making her way back towards her dressing room. She didn't get far, though, before she was distracted by the very loud noise of the studio's main gate as it opened and scraped over the uneven concrete floor. Bela turned around to see who it was.

'Shashi *sahib's* here, Shashi *sahib's* here,' whispered the unit members to one another. It was Monica's dad.

Curious, Bela watched as a shiny black stretch limousine crawled into the studio forecourt. Shashi stepped out of the car wearing a plain white suit, white mock-croc shoes and a huge pair of gold-rimmed sunglasses. Bela and Marc looked at each other. Marc raised an eyebrow and Bela wanted to burst out laughing. Apparently, Shashi Kumar hadn't bought a single item of clothing since his heyday in the 1970s.

Bela looked intently at his face but she barely recognised him. She had seen quite a few of the mushy masala movies he had churned out, but he looked quite different now. Shashi Kumar had lost a fair amount of his hair and had gained a portly belly instead. He indicated to his driver to open the back door of the car and, one by one, a dozen or so schoolchildren emerged wearing dark green and grey uniforms.

'Hello Shashi *sahib*,' said Yogi, politely greeting him with a double-handed handshake. 'What can we get you? Rimpu, go get some water and order tea for Shashi *sahib*,' he shouted out to his assistant.

It was very clear that Shashi Kumar was boss.

'Where's Monica?' he asked Yogi. 'These children have come from a school where I was attending a fundraising event. They won a talent competition and the first prize was a visit to the studio. I promised them a tour of the set and a meeting with Monica to get her autograph.'

'Papa, Papa!' Monica came running through an open door at the other end of the studio and gave her dad a big hug. Immediately a little old lady got out of the car and opened up a big umbrella to shelter Monica from the strong rays of the sun.

In an instant, Monica was surrounded by the excited schoolchildren as they formed a huge circle around her and demanded her autograph. As she signed, more people started running towards the studio from the road outside, trying to get into the enclosure. The security guards had forgotten to close the gate and at least a dozen more people made their way inside.

'Shut the gate!' screamed Shashi Kumar to the security guards. 'What kind of idiot security are you? My daughter's in here, I want maximum protection at all times! Full alert, do you hear me?'

Bela stood back and watched everything that was going on around her. She was especially interested to see how protective Shashi Kumar was over his daughter.

Marc's phone rang and he strode away to take the call. At the same time, Micky hurried back on to the set with Bela's mobile. 'You left this on the table,' he said, out of breath. 'It keeps ringing, and it's driving me nuts!'

It wasn't long before everyone on the set found out why. On cue Bela's phone went off again and it was really loud. The children instantly looked around to see where the noisy bhangra tune was coming from. Once they realised whose phone it was, there was no holding them back. They rushed forward to meet Bela, who hurriedly switched her phone off.

'It's Bela, it's Bela!' yelled the kids, even more excited than before. 'Bela, please give us your autograph,' they begged, holding their scraps of paper up towards her. Now *she* was suddenly surrounded by dozens of expectant faces.

The children were dancing around her, bouncing up and down, and even the adults who had managed to sneak in were unashamedly thrusting their pens and bits of paper forward. Those who didn't have any paper were asking for her scribble on their hands.

Over by the limousine, Monica was left standing with just a pen in her hand and her umbrella-holding lady. She flashed an envious look at Bela and then got into the car and disappeared behind the blacked-out windows. The tyres screeched as the car sped out of the studio.

'Did you see that?' Micky asked Bela in a hushed tone. 'She did *not* look happy. Everyone's raving about you these days and talking about how you've come from nowhere to become such a big name. Maybe she's starting to believe what she's hearing – that she's no longer Queen Bee – or an A-lister.'

'Oh don't be mean, Micky,' said Bela. 'I feel bad enough about that stupid article as it is. And we don't need things to get any worse between us considering I'm shooting with her from tomorrow. What joy!'

Chapter 2

'Ohhhhhh!' groaned Bela. She buried her face firmly under the duvet as her alarm clock rang out. It was 4am. 'No-one should have to get up at such an ungodly hour,' she thought as she fumbled around, looking for the snooze button on the clock before remembering there wasn't one.

Bela's alarm clock, which was a plastic model of herself, was a gift from her brother Reuben. He was at university in London and had found it on a stall on Southall Broadway. It hammered out a tune from Bela's debut movie and although it was really tacky, it amazed her to think she was so well-known that such a thing existed. Plus, it was so loud it never failed to get her out of bed.

'That mad clock must be waking the whole neighbourhood up as well,' said Bela's mum, Sheila, as she popped her head round the door of Bela's bedroom. 'It certainly put an end to my nice dream.'

'Sorry, Mum.'

'Never mind. I wanted to talk to you anyway. I wanted to remind you not to start blabbing to any reporters today. You're too nice, that's your problem,' she muttered as she wandered over to the window to peer outside. 'Next time you have an interview, I'm going to come with you so I can make sure you say what you're supposed to say. I should be on set with you at all times, but you never let me come.'

'It's just my job, Mum. You don't need to be there.'

'I don't agree. You're too independent nowadays, you young girls. That's why you get into all this trouble.' Sheila had always complained about Bela not taking her along to shoots, but Bela was adamant about going alone. She didn't want to be like the other actresses who couldn't move a muscle without mummy's say-so – and there were plenty of them. She also didn't want her mum to be seen as a pushy parent; there were plenty of those, too.

'Oh Mum, please. Not now,' said Bela, stretching. 'Let me at least have a cup of tea before you start. In any case, I haven't been blabbing to journalists. I'm not that stupid!'

'Hmmm.'

'What do you mean by that Ma? These magazines just make things up as they go along. Reuben keeps calling, too,' she added, rubbing her eyes. 'I missed three calls on my mobile yesterday. Dad says he phoned here a couple of times as well.'

'I know.'

'So you've obviously been talking to him about the whole "Star Wars" thing as well,' Bela sighed.

'Yes, well I had to say something, didn't I? He was wondering how his sweet little sister had managed to get into all the bitchy gossip columns!'

'Well, if he calls here again today while I'm out, tell him I'll chat to him online when I get back,' Bela instructed as she started to haul herself out of bed.

'Anything you say, Madam. I'll pass your message on. By the way, you look awful,' she stated as she left the room. 'Sleep a bit more.'

Bela was just about to rush to the mirror to see what her mum meant, when her phone rang. It was Jaya, Bela's agent. 'Hi Jaya, I'm just getting ready. Don't worry, I'll be there on time.'

'That's not why I'm phoning, Bela,' said Jaya, with a note of urgency in her voice. 'I know you probably haven't done anything wrong, but keep away from Monica,' she warned.

'What do you mean?' asked Bela.

'Just do your job and don't get involved in anything but acting. That girl's got connections so let's just say you don't want to get on the wrong side of her or her dad. If you're not careful, you'll get a reputation as a troublesome and arrogant actress. And that will affect your whole career.'

Bela was a bit taken aback by Jaya's direct and formal tone. Did she also think Bela had been talking to journalists? Or did she know something Bela didn't? Either way, Bela didn't quite like the sound of it, and she was just about to tell Jaya that she wouldn't say anything she shouldn't, but didn't get a chance as Jaya abruptly hung up.

As she chucked her phone down on the bed, though, Bela decided she wasn't going to let her moody agent or even the thought of working alongside Monica dampen her spirits. She was looking forward to the day ahead as she would be filming what was already being billed as the hit song of the year. The three heroines – Bela, Monica and Deepa – and their heroes, played by Marc Fernandez, Ajay Banerjee and Sanjay Suri, were to film a wedding song sequence that would appear towards the interval of a film called *Mumbai Magic*.

Just the thought of seeing Marc's dashing face again was enough to send Bela skipping happily around the room, so twenty minutes and a cup of steaming, sweet masala tea later, Bela was sitting pretty in the back seat of her chauffeur-driven car.

'Morning, Raju, how are you doing?' Bela asked her driver chirpily as they made their way to Blockbuster Studios.

'Fine *didi*,' Raju replied politely. 'How's your mum?'

'Yeah, she's normal, if you know what I mean,' said Bela. 'Mums are mums, always moaning about something or other.'

'Very true,' laughed Raju.

'Mind you, I guess she's just concerned about me. Some odd things have been happening recently, but I'm not quite sure what to make of it all… Raju, have you heard any stories about me and Monica?

The whole of the film industry seems to think we hate each other, but what about you? What do you think?'

'Well, I don't know if it's true or not, but I did read some stuff about you two being rivals and who thinks who's better than the other,' Raju answered. 'But I can't say I know all the ins and outs of it, or how it started. Maybe you can fill me in?'

'Thanks, that's really interesting,' Bela said, yawning. 'It's way too early in the day to go into detail now but I'll tell you all about it later. Just don't believe everything you hear, okay?'

'Okay *didi*,' he said.

Raju was only three years older than Bela and she'd known him all her life. His mum had worked as a cleaner for Bela's parents from the very day that Bela was born. Bela had always wanted to do something more for the family and as soon as she was signed up for her first movie, she offered Raju a full-time job. It was accepted with much gratitude.

'I just hope the journos don't ask me anything about her,' said Bela, talking more to herself than Raju. 'I don't want to say bad things about Monica, but I don't particularly want to say nicer things either as I'm not sure she is nice.'

'It's sometimes best not to say anything at all,'

advised Raju. 'Silence is golden, right?'

'Yeah, I guess I'll have to stay away from them or keep it strictly professional,' agreed Bela. 'If I'm asked, perhaps I'll just say she's a good actress, which she is. Kind of.'

'Do you ever get angry about any of the stuff that's written about you?' asked Raju, glancing at Bela through his rear-view mirror.

'Well, I'm getting a bit annoyed about having to explain myself to everyone all the time – including my mum,' Bela replied, rolling her eyes. 'But I'm not angry because I don't know who to be angry at. Monica can't be to blame because most of the stories are quite negative about her too, so it must be the journalists.'

'But who's giving them the info?' he asked.

'I haven't got a clue and frankly, I think it's getting boring. I'd rather read about Marc's workout regime than this nonsense,' she laughed.

'It might be boring for you, Bela *didi*, but the fans love this kind of stuff. And who knows, maybe the gossip mags are the reason you're such a star – maybe it's not just due to your good looks and talent.' He winked cheekily as they pulled up into the car park of the film studio.

'Ha, that's funny,' said Bela as she got out of the

car. 'But I seriously hope you're wrong.'

It was a chilly morning so Bela grabbed her fluffy pink shawl from the back seat and wrapped it snugly around her. As she approached the set, she could see it was already a hive of activity and the unit members were dashing around frantically, trying to get every detail right for this important scene.

The set, made up like a luxurious living room in a huge mansion, looked fantastic with its colourful backdrop of gold, red and brown fairy lights. It was clear that a lot of time and attention had been given to the detail, and Bela thought the rich, dark wood furniture with its bright silk upholstery really hit the mark.

She looked around to see if any of the other actors had arrived, but she seemed to be the first. After politely waving at all the spot boys and assistants – whose eyes, she noticed, had been fixed on her beautiful face from the very moment she arrived – Bela quietly made her way to the dance studio to see if the film's choreographer, Kiran Patel, was there. Kiran was a very experienced and well-respected dance master, but this was the first time Bela would have the chance to work with her.

'Hey Bela,' said Kiran, glancing up. She was busily putting out dance mats in preparation for another film shoot later in the day. 'You're bright and early.'

'Early maybe, but bright – definitely not,' said Bela. 'What I could have done for a lie-in this morning.'

'Yeah, but it'll be worth it when you've done the song,' said Kiran, brushing away the dust that had gathered on her black jogging bottoms. 'This is gonna be one of the big hits of the year when the film's released, I'm telling you. I knew it the second I heard it – people on the set are already humming the tune.'

'I know. It's infectious,' commented Bela. 'I can't get it out of my head either.'

'With a bit of luck, it should catch on with the masses as well, not to mention the dance routines. You're a lucky girl fronting this one,' smiled Kiran. 'Let's have a quick run-through.'

Kiran moved over to the small silver CD player that was perched on the window sill. 'I've put together some moves and I want to see if they work for you.'

Bela eagerly removed her shawl and her shoes, then dumped her belongings in one corner of the huge room. Kiran turned on the CD player and pressed play. She came and stood directly in front of Bela and began showing her the moves for the first verse.

Kiran was a dab hand at this job. She had the ability to make up brilliant moves on the spot. In fact, she refused to rehearse songs beforehand at all. She just turned up on a movie set and decided what steps she would use on the very day they were being filmed. Kiran claimed that the music told her what to do.

Bela watched in awe as Kiran demonstrated the nifty moves she had just composed. Then it was Bela's turn. She relaxed her shoulders by forming small circular movements, waited for the music to start, and then began. As soon as Bela started to dance, her face lit up. As she mimed to the romantic lyrics her expressions came to life and you could tell she was really enjoying herself. In fact, Kiran found it hard to believe this was the same sleepy-looking girl who had tip-toed into the dance studio a few moments before.

Bela's hands moved with real grace, and as she twirled around she kept her eyes on her imaginary hero. Her feet moved fast but her movements were always coordinated and she was so delicate in her performance that she was a delight to watch.

'Wow, that's great!' said Kiran, clapping. 'You're a

natural, obviously. Yeah, I'd heard about your dancing having that something special. You won some competition, didn't you?' she asked. 'That's how you got into the movies?'

Bela nodded, impressed by Kiran's knowledge of her background and very flattered. She was a real fan of Kiran's work and knew that the choreographer was the genius behind a whole load of hit films.

'Okay, Bela, let's carry on with me at the front and you behind. Just copy. Ready 1, 2, 3…'

Kiran played the CD from the beginning of the main verse again and Bela followed, move for move, with almost the same efficiency and poise. Her body flowed effortlessly along with the music, and it was obvious to Kiran that Bela loved dancing.

'Brilliant,' commended Kiran once they had finished the verse. 'I can see I don't have to worry about you.'

'Thanks,' smiled Bela, delighted with the vote of confidence.

'It's cold outside so wait here and I'll see if the crew's ready for us. There are loads of extras to deal with today – it's gonna be a long, difficult session.'

Just as Kiran was making her way out of the room the floor manager of the film, Jagdish, walked in. 'Where are you going, Kiran?' he asked.

'Just checking to see if everyone's here,' she replied. 'Are we ready to go?'

'Yes, they're all here… they're just having a quick cup of tea in the reception area. Everyone's already been briefed,' he said. 'Which is why I'm here.'

Jagdish turned to look at Bela, who was still standing bare-footed in the middle of the room. 'We're going to make a slight change to the schedule my sweetie,' he began.

Bela bristled. She knew straight away that this wasn't good news. Jagdish never spoke so politely unless he needed a favour. His nickname was Jolly Jags, but this was ironic. Usually his manner was very curt and abrupt.

Jagdish had a small square face with a thick black moustache and he always seemed to be frowning. He was one of those people who would never look someone in the eye when he spoke to them. He would gaze over their shoulder or at his feet, and it made whoever he was talking to feel very uncomfortable.

Bela stared directly at him but his eyes darted around the room. Jagdish paused to cough as he was about to speak and Bela could tell he was nervous. 'Uhh, producer *sahib* – Dev*ji* –thinks it will be better for the film if Marc and Monica are the main focus of the wedding song,' he announced, stroking down both sides of his moustache with one hand.

Bela looked at Kiran with disbelief.

Jagdish took a few steps towards Bela and then stopped. He looked up at the ceiling and then back down, shuffling his feet anxiously, while Bela waited for him to produce an explanation.

Jagdish had a small build and was wearing a white half-sleeved shirt with black trousers that were definitely too short and he completed the look with black, plastic flip-flops. In any other situation Bela would have found it hard to take him seriously, but this was no joke. She just didn't know what to say.

'But we've rehearsed the song already and Bela's doing a great job,' Kiran declared, realising that Bela needed some help. 'I created the steps with her in mind as I was told she's classically trained. We've had a run-through and Bela's quite brilliant. Monica's okay, but she moves differently. She's better suited to modern numbers. Her hips don't move in the same way – it won't work,' she finished.

'Look, I'm just the messenger and I've been told that the decision's been made. That's it,' stated Jagdish very assertively, ending all possibility of negotiation. 'The production house wants Monica to take the lead – no offence, Bela,' he concluded, looking in Bela's direction but not directly at her.

'I'd like to speak to Dev *sahib*,' said Bela, fighting back tears of disappointment and anger. 'This isn't fair. He can't just change everything around. What about the script? The song's supposed to focus on me and Marc, as he's my romantic lead. It won't work if he's dancing with just anyone.'

'He won't be dancing with "just anyone",' Jagdish fired back. 'He'll be dancing with Monica, and in the story Monica has the hots for him even though she's dating Ajay. So, you see, it works.'

'But–' Bela didn't get a chance to finish what she was about to say as Jagdish interrupted.

'All this has been thought through – you don't need to worry about it,' he continued. 'It's for the betterment of the film, I assure you. Anyhow, Dev*ji* is out of town and can't be reached for two days. We have to complete this by tomorrow or we'll fall seriously behind schedule. We have a hundred extras on hire for two full days and the agency is due to bring them all here, fully dressed in an hour. We're going ahead with it this way, Bela.'

Bela felt utterly forlorn. She wished she had someone to turn to, but who? She couldn't call Reuben in the middle of the English night, and she didn't want to bother her mother and make her worry even more. She could call Jaya but after this morning's phone conversation Bela wasn't sure she'd be on her side anyway.

Her brain was whirring, but she knew she was cornered. Jagdish had presented the situation as a done deal and she had no choice but to agree. Otherwise she would be the cause of a major scheduling problem and would be seen as the villain of the piece.

'I'll walk out of the movie, Bela, if that's what you want, darling,' said Kiran supportively, realising that Bela didn't know what to do. 'I'll back you one hundred per cent. You're right, it's not fair. This isn't film-making, it's politics.'

'Don't be silly Kiran*ji*,' said Bela considerately. 'You can't walk out on my account. I guess I have no choice. If I kick up a fuss, we'll lose two days of shooting and it won't be fair on the rest of the cast. If they don't want me for the song, what can I do? They simply don't want me…' her voice trailed off.

Seeing Bela was weakening and was almost ready to succumb, Jagdish piped up. 'You and Deepa will still be in the song, singing and dancing as planned. It's just the verse you don't need to worry about. Oh, and your outfit is *absolutely wow*, Bela.

41

I've just had a sneak preview. You'll look just like Geeta Begum, my all-time favourite actress.'

Kiran wasn't impressed. She was very angry with Jagdish, firstly for his emotional blackmail, and now for trying to make out that it didn't matter who got the main verses of the song. Kiran had worked in the film industry for fifteen years and had come across these scenarios before, but she felt really upset on this particular occasion. Bela was definitely a better dancer than Monica and, quite apart from the unfairness, this meant that Kiran's job would now be harder and the results not quite as good.

'So, Jagdish, you mean to tell me this has nothing to do with the fact that the producer of this movie is Shashi Kumar's buddy?' Kiran had decided it was best to be blunt about what was going on here. 'Is this change really because it's better for the script or just because you're all trying to please Monica's dad?'

'The decision has nothing to do with you,' Jagdish retorted venomously, 'and you don't have the right to question it. You're just a choreographer – that's your job, so stick to it. If the producer tells you to make a monkey dance, then that's what you do.'

Kiran was shocked. Jagdish had gone too far. Here she was – a well-regarded and well-known professional – being insulted by someone who was little more than a lackey. She was fuming. Without any hesitation, she took two giant strides forward and gave Jagdish a big, hard slap across the right side of his face. *Thaah!* The large, empty studio amplified the sound of Kiran's strike.

Bela winced. She could almost feel the stinging pain that Jagdish was feeling.

Jagdish himself just stood there for a moment and held his cheek, which had turned very red. He looked ready to explode but, somehow keeping a lid on his temper, he gave Kiran a menacing stare. 'You'll pay for this. You'll pay,' he threatened.

Kiran stared back at him, unflinching. It was more dramatic than a scene from a Bollywood film itself.

Jagdish then turned his back to Kiran and walked off, his flip-flops slapping the floor in anger. He tried to slam the swing doors behind him, but they just floated silently closed.

Bela forgot her own disappointment for a few moments as her feelings for Kiran took over. Kiran was an incredible talent with countless successful films to her name. She didn't deserve to be insulted for speaking out. Bela was also humbled by the knowledge that Kiran had been ready to fight for her. It meant a lot.

Then, just when it seemed there couldn't be any more drama in the studio, Marc suddenly burst in. 'What's all this I hear?' he asked, looking at Bela, then Kiran, and then Bela again. 'I've just got in and I've been told Bela's been sidelined in the wedding scene. Is that true?'

Bela looked down. *Sidelined.* That word felt like a dagger to her heart. Jagdish could disguise it however he wanted, but that was the truth of the matter. She had been sidelined.

Bela no longer cared that the best looking man in the world was standing in front of her. She just wanted to go home, crawl into her bed and cry her heart out.

'Favours,' Kiran told Marc, frankly. 'Favours, politics, call it what you want. We all know what's going on here. I told Bela I'd go on strike for her, but then she agreed to go along with their plan. It wasn't really her fault she backed down, though. She was blackmailed.'

'You agreed to the change?' Marc asked Bela, sounding rather surprised. 'You shouldn't have done that, Bela. I've got nothing against Monica, but it's supposed to be the big song of the film and it's unfair to snatch it away from you like that. You should have stuck to your guns – you have a contract, they can't do this if you won't let them.'

Bela decided she didn't want any more sympathy because then she really would start crying.

'Thanks for the support,' she mumbled, turning her face away so Marc wouldn't notice the tears welling up in her eyes. She went to pick up her shawl and her bag which were lying in the corner of the room. 'If they want Monica, there's not much I can do,' she added, trying to be as unemotional about it as she could. 'But thanks, anyway…'

She put her shoes on, draped her bag and shawl over one shoulder and walked out of the room.

For the first time in her brief career, Bela felt her age – a tender sixteen years old. She wished her mum was with her and wondered whether the lead song would have been snatched away if she had been. Today, the hard way, she realised her mum may have been right. Perhaps Bela was trying to become too independent too soon.

Once she got back to the set, she joined the other members of the main cast who were standing together, watching the production crew set up the shot. There were many more people around now and it was very noisy. Bela made sure she didn't catch anyone's eye as she didn't want to talk about what had just happened.

A few moments later Marc came and stood beside Bela, as if to show his support but neither of them said a word. He looked more serious than usual; he wasn't laughing or joking around. Bela was certain that Kiran must have filled him in on why she hadn't kicked up a fuss.

Monica was sitting on the bottom step of the false staircase that formed a part of the huge set. She was casually chatting away to someone on her mobile phone and Bela looked straight at her, hoping she would show some kind of emotion to indicate whether she had engineered this situation or not. But Monica's body language gave nothing away.

Jagdish began yelling for everyone to pay attention and get into position. Kiran moved to the front to face the crowd and stood with a loudspeaker. 'This is just a run-through, so don't worry about outfits and make-up yet,' she shouted. 'Marc, Monica, to the front. Deepa, Bela, Ajay and Sanjay, get behind.'

Bela and Marc took a few steps towards the gathered people on the set and as Marc moved to the front of the crowd, Bela shifted behind. Deepa sidled up to her, but Bela didn't look her way. Instead, she took in the scene in front of her. Kiran began showing Monica and Marc the very dance moves Bela had just been practising. It hurt.

At that moment, Bela decided that although she felt powerless to do anything about the wedding dance she would make sure something like this never happened again. Bela quietly broke away from the group and went up to Jagdish.

'Contact producer *sahib* and tell him I'd like a meeting with him as soon as he gets back in town,' she said in a hushed, but firm manner. My agent, Jaya, will also be present.'

Bela would tell the film's producer, Dev Dhillon, that this would be the one and only scene in the film where she'd compromise. If they tried to force any other changes on her she would walk out of the production.

Chapter 3

Two weeks had passed since the unpleasant *Mumbai Magic* song incident and Bela had finally managed to put the sorry saga out of her mind. It hadn't been easy though.

She could still hardly believe how the central song and dance sequence of the film had been so cruelly stolen from her at the last minute. Bela had

had to watch Monica – of all people – lip-synching to lyrics that she had come to see as her own. And to top it all, the smug look on Monica's face as she joyously twirled around with Marc really infuriated her.

Thankfully, in a city like Mumbai life moves so fast that there is little time to dwell on such 'unpleasantnesses' as Bela called them. And she was still very much in demand. She was invited to be chief guest at the opening ceremony of a fancy new restaurant called City Lights, she signed up for two more big-banner movies, and was now getting ready to be whisked off to Rajasthan to shoot the climax of a historical movie entitled *Mera Maharajah*.

The Maharajah was being played by young teen idol Ajay Banerjee, and Bela was to play the part of a courtesan. Bela was already working alongside Ajay in *Mumbai Magic*, and although she didn't know him all that well, she found him to be very friendly and approachable. Ajay was only five feet and eight inches tall but his cute looks, flawless complexion and floppy brown hair had made him a schoolgirl pin-up.

For her part, Bela considered this to be a really challenging role as it was different from the typical girl-meets-boy-to-fall-in-love-despite-family-opposition parts. And she was really keyed up about shooting in Rajasthan. She had never been to the regal Indian state before, and they'd be filming at the Water Palace, which was a breathtaking gold and marble building situated in the middle of Lake Raj.

'I just can't wait. Yippppeeeee!' typed Bela, chatting to her brother Reuben online the night before travelling.

'And guess wot? Tara is coming with me. Can't believe I managed that. I just asked director if I could take a mate along as it was my first major outdoor shoot away from my family and he said yes!!!!'

'Great,' replied Reuben.

'But b careful. Tara's a bit mad. Knowing her, she prob only goin cos she fancies Ajay. Don't get caught up in stuff with her. She's a liability. Focus on the job! Txt me when u get there. Reuben XX'

Bela hadn't felt this excited in a long time. She had even packed her cases three nights in advance. Since she didn't get to spend much time with her friends any more, this trip was just what Bela needed to inject some girlie fun back into her life. And there was no better person to do that with than Tara.

* * *

'Oh my goodness, look at that! It's bloody amazing!' Tara squealed with delight when they arrived at the historic Water Palace.

Bela agreed. The majestic gold and white building rose out of the peaceful water of the lake and stood so proudly against the striking red sky. It was a sight to behold.

'First the private jet and now this… I'm still flying!' exclaimed Tara, squeezing Bela's arm with excitement.

The girls gathered together with the rest of the cast and crew in the hotel lobby while porters fetched the luggage from the private taxis that had ferried them from the airport. After a few minutes the hotel manager informed Bela and Tara that they'd be staying in the Rani Room of the Palace's residential quarters.

'So, where's Ajay gonna be staying?' Tara asked Bela, with a naughty look on her face.

Bela elbowed her in a friendly manner and whispered, 'You'd better behave yourself, Madam. Seriously, it's my reputation on the line. No-one here knows you and if you start causing trouble they're just going to remember you're my friend.'

'Oh you never know,' Tara replied cockily. 'I've got a way of leaving my own mark wherever I go.'

Bela was a bit concerned for a moment – you never quite knew what Tara was capable of – but she was distracted by a porter who grabbed their cases and began loading them up on to a large metal trolley. Tara only had a small suitcase, a rather tatty-looking blue thing, but Bela had brought three huge silver-coloured cases along because she'd had to carry with her all the outfits she needed for the shoot.

The porter, dressed in full Rajasthani finery, led the way and once they reached the room he opened the door. Neither Bela nor Tara could quite believe their eyes. It was the most luxurious, sumptuous hotel suite you could ever imagine. It was decorated in rich Rajasthani colours – burnt oranges, yellows and reds – and featured exquisite handcrafted wooden furniture carved with intricate designs.

There was a gorgeous chaise longue on one side of the room and on the other stood two huge double beds with plump silk cushions. In the far corner by the window was a big desk complete with computer and internet connection.

Tara dived on to the chaise longue and kicked her legs in delight. 'This is *sooooo* cool! Seriously, it's fit for a queen – Queen Tara of Rajapur,' she joked. 'I still can't believe how you got to here, Bela. You're so lucky!'

Bela smiled, but didn't say anything. At times like this, she too could hardly believe how lucky she was to be experiencing things she could only have dreamed about a few years before. 'It's the stuff of rajahs and maharajahs,' she thought to herself.

'Mind you,' said Tara, moving from the chaise longue and throwing herself on to one of the big, plush beds. 'You probably deserve it after all the stuff that's happened with that Monicow. Oops!' she laughed. 'Now that really was a Freudian slip. But it's a great name, so that's what I'll call her from now.'

'You're so bad, Tara. You haven't changed one bit have you?' said Bela, removing her shoes. 'But we're not supposed to be talking about her, remember? We're here for a break and some fun.'

'Oh yeah, I'd forgotten that's why I'm here – to help you forget about Moo-nica. Is that better?' Tara asked mischievously.

Bela laughed. There was no point in trying to tame Tara, she was always going to do and say as she pleased. But that's why Bela liked her so much – Tara always spoke her mind.

The two friends unpacked their clothes, then called room service and ordered their gourmet banquet, all the while gossiping and giggling about anything and everything. Bela was really enjoying herself but knew that it couldn't be like this for the whole of the four-day stint.

'As much as I'd like to carry on chatting all night, I've got to go to bed,' she said, forcing her mind back to her work. 'I've got to get up at five am, Tara. That's when the make-up woman's coming.'

'As long as you don't disturb me,' said Tara, crawling under the duvet, 'I don't care what time you have to be up.'

* * *

Sure enough, at five the next morning Bela's appointed stylist tapped on the door. Bela didn't mind, though. She was looking forward to getting dressed up again. The old courtesan outfits were extremely elaborate and her costumes for this film were fabulous.

Bela had to wear so many different types of jewels – for her hair, body, upper arms, ankles and feet – and so much heavy, specialist make-up, that it took three hours to complete her mesmerising look.

She was on set at nine and the filming schedule was so intense she didn't get back to her room until eight in the evening – after sunset. This was the case for the second day, too. It wasn't quite the girlie holiday Bela had hoped for, but she was enjoying herself all the same.

Tara didn't seem to mind either. She usually slept in until mid-day and then kept herself busy, either by watching the shoot or going to the local markets with Ajay Banerjee's mum.

Ajay's mum had come along to the film shoot purely because she had always wanted to stay at the fabulous Water Palace. She did get slightly bored during the long breaks in between shots, though, and seemed to be glad to have a fellow chatterbox and shopaholic like Tara to hang out with.

Tara, for her part, was spending time with Ajay's mum hoping that if she played her cards right she might be calling her 'mum' by the end of the week too. It was a tall order, but the girl loved challenges.

By the third day of the shoot, Bela was fully immersed in her character. For the very first time in her career she was moved by her role. She wondered why she'd never stopped to think about courtesans before; how ill-regarded they were by society and how tragic and lonely their lives were. 'It's amazing, isn't it, Tara, how these girls were forced to dance, and how tough their lives were? They had to entertain all those filthy rich men just to survive,' said Bela during the lunch break.

All around them, members of the crew were hungrily wolfing down masala dosas, a South Indian speciality ordered by the production team. But Bela didn't have food on her mind. She went on, 'These poor girls gave men pleasure by entertaining them but were then scorned by the majority of people. I'm not even sure if they had real relationships with these men at all, or whether they just danced for them, or if it was a bit of both. It'd be fascinating to find out.'

Tara obviously didn't think so. Bela could see her eyes glazing over. This type of conversation was way too deep for her. Tara was bored and couldn't be bothered to pretend she was interested. She was busily looking around for someone.

'What's up Tara? Who are you looking for?' Bela enquired, giving her friend a knowing glance.

'Ajay, that's who,' said Tara frankly. 'Trouble is, I don't think he's even noticed me – and I've been hanging around and entertaining his mum for three whole days.'

'What do you expect, Tara? He's working, not looking for a wife!' laughed Bela.

'Well, there's nothing stopping him from killing two birds with one stone, is there?' responded Tara rather hopefully. 'Nothing's going my way at the moment,' she moaned. 'I've even tried to smile and catch the eye of the film director a few times, hoping that he'll find a role for me in the movie, but that doesn't seem to be working either.'

'Tara, he can't just create a role for you like that, crazy girl! That's not how it works.'

'Well, it's his loss,' said Tara, turning her nose up in the air. 'I'm going for a wander. See you back in the room.'

Once the shoot was over, Bela went straight to the Rani Room to remove the heavy make-up and even heavier garments she was wearing. She was surprised to see there was no sign of Tara, but she showered, changed and then headed off to the restaurant area to look for her.

As Bela approached the restaurant, she could hear whooping and loud laughter, which was unusual as it was normally a very quiet and formal dining room. When she reached the entrance, Bela saw that a crowd had gathered in the middle of the dining hall. She walked over to where the people were standing, thinking it must be a comedy act put on by the Palace, but she couldn't see what was going on and couldn't hear much because of all the laughter. She politely squeezed her way past a few people to get closer to the front.

Bela got the shock of her life when she saw that the comedian in action was none other than Tara. The daring girl was standing up on a table, belting out dialogues from old Hindi movies and impersonating some of the most popular actors, old and new.

Most of the diners had left their tables to get a closer view of Tara's performance and the waiters had temporarily abandoned their jobs to enjoy the show. They were all in stitches.

Bela darted over to Tara and tugged at her jeans from behind. 'Tara, what the hell are you doing?' asked Bela, concerned that they could both get into a lot of trouble for this.

'*Hai hai*,' responded Tara, in a mock-coy tone. 'It's lovely little Bela.'

Bela realised then that there was no stopping her friend. Tara had always loved attention and here she was, centre-stage. 'My name is Bela,' mocked Tara, fluttering her eyelashes. 'You must all know that I am just *soooooo* sweet. I've worked my way up to the top, and I'd still never say anything bad about anyone… even Monica…'

Bela gasped and the audience burst out laughing. Tara carried on. 'Monica's okay… for a B-lister… just remember I'm number one and she's number two...'

The audience was in hysterics again. Bela didn't know whether to laugh or cry. She was surprised to see that everyone understood the sketch and that they found it so funny. Some were even recording Tara's act on their mobile phones.

A few people noticed that Bela was there, but that didn't stop them from chuckling. Even Bela couldn't help smiling because Tara had got the mannerisms so right.

'And now, Ladies and Gentlemen, for my final performance,' announced Tara, with much pomp.

Bela looked on, frightened to think what might be coming next. Tara put on a sultry pout and struck a model pose, flicking her hair away from her face with real style.

'Hi guys… I need no introduction of course, as everyone knows me, but my name's Monica…'

The guys started wolf-whistling and Tara carried on striking sexy poses.

'My dad is the famous Shashi Kumar and as you

must know, he owns Bollywood. My mum was a star too. Bollywood is in my blood. In fact, my blood sings and dances as it travels through my veins.'

Everyone was laughing really hard by this stage. It was a stupid sketch but Tara's voice, movements and style mimicked Monica so perfectly that you couldn't help being amused. Tara carried on pouting, the guys carried on whistling and, by now, Bela was in fits of laughter.

It was only when the hotel manager found out what was going on and rushed into the dining hall that Tara ended the impromptu show by leaping off the table and hiding behind Bela. The waiters hurried back inside the kitchen, the diners strolled back to their tables and Bela and Tara giggled all the way back to their room to bed.

* * *

The next morning, once again, Bela left for work before Tara was up. It was the final day of filming and Bela was feeling slightly wistful as she had really enjoyed her stay in Rajasthan. Most of the cast had already gone back to Mumbai since they weren't needed any more, and there were just a handful of people on set now.

Ajay's mum was sitting on the sidelines having a

cup of tea, and she gestured to Bela to go over and speak to her. 'I've been hearing all about Tara the comedian,' she told Bela. 'I would never have guessed that's she's an impressionist. Where is she?'

Bela smiled, unsure whether Ajay's mum was joking or really thought Tara was a professional mimic. Before she could say anything, though, Ajay, who was standing close by, came and sat beside his mum.

'I didn't see the live performance either,' he said to Bela. 'I wouldn't have had your friend down as an entertainer but she was the talk of the restaurant at breakfast. Someone's even gone to the bother of putting her sketches on the internet, on VideoWeb. Once we're done here, we can go and have a look.'

'What?' asked Bela, amazed. 'VideoWeb? Oh my goodness, how hilarious! How did it get on the net?' As the words left her mouth, though, Bela remembered the onlookers who had been filming Tara on their mobiles.

'Apparently, if you type in "Water Palace" it comes straight up,' said Ajay, sipping his frothy coffee.

Bela was very keen to see Tara in action on the internet, but her next shot had already been set up. It was two hours before there was a break in filming and she was able to rush back to her bedroom.

'Tara, Tara, get up! You're famous!'

Tara peered groggily over the top of her duvet, rubbing her eyes. 'Uhh? What?'

'Someone's put your late-night impersonations on VideoWeb. Ajay was telling me…'

Suddenly Tara found the energy to get out of bed. She scrambled out, her hair a tangled mess, and rushed over to sit beside Bela who switched the machine on. When the VideoWeb web page loaded, Bela typed "Water Palace" into the search box and, immediately, a list of results popped up. Right at the very top was one that read: "Water Palace – girl mimics Bela".

'Looks as though you *have* made your mark, Tara, just as you predicted when we first got here! Who would have thought?'

Tara cupped one hand anxiously over her mouth as Bela played the clip. Within seconds, though, they were both laughing again.

'I am not at all like that Tara Mehta,' said Bela, placing her hands on her hips as she watched her friend aping her. 'I shouldn't even be finding this funny, but the faces you pull are so hilarious,' she added as the video came to an end.

'Let's see if there's any more,' said Tara, excitedly.

As Bela scrolled down the list again, her eyes stopped at one particular search result. 'What's this?' she exclaimed, pointing at the screen.

Tara began to read: 'Bela laughs at "Monica".'

'Oh no!' said Bela, feeling a little bit sick. She clicked on the link. 'What have you done?'

The recording began with a brief shot of Tara pouting and posing as Monica. The camera then panned in on Bela's face which showed her clapping and laughing uncontrollably at Tara's impersonation. When you looked at it this way, completely out of context, Bela knew it seemed as though she was encouraging Tara's mockery of Monica and that she was enjoying it the most.

The two girls looked at one another, aghast. Suddenly, the joke was on them.

* * *

Back in Mumbai, despite some people interpreting the VideoWeb clip as evidence of Bela's disdain for Monica, Bela decided she wouldn't let it get her down. She'd had a good telling off from both her mum and her agent, Jaya, but Bela refused to let this minor PR disaster mar the good memories of her time in Rajasthan.

She was going to turn her attention to positive

things, and right now nothing could be more exciting than the biggest event of the year – the *FilmGlitz* Magazine Awards party.

'I'm *sooooo* excited about tonight!' Bela said to Reuben on the phone. 'This is *the* party to be at. All the stars turn up. I still can't believe that I'm nominated for two awards – and for one of them, I'm up against Monica. It's mad.'

''Course it's bloody mad. I thought you were gonna end up as a schoolteacher,' said Reuben, who was delighted for her. 'I'm getting loads of extra attention because of you. The guys all hang around in the hope that I might introduce them to you one day and the girls are always asking stupid questions like whether you and Monica really hate each other. It's hilarious.'

The siblings laughed as they went on to discuss Tara's infamous impersonations. Bela was glad that her brother could see the funny side of it and didn't think Bela deserved all the negative publicity. She was pleased to be talking to Reuben but felt sad that they were missing out on so much of each other's lives. He was busy with his studies and she had no time for holidays, so they hadn't met for six long months.

As soon as Bela ended the call, her phone rang

again. This time, it was another one of her school friends, Priyanka.

'Oh my God!' Priyanka began when Bela answered. She was clearly excited about something.

'I've heard you're gonna be performing on stage with Marc tonight at the awards. True?' she pressed, and then, without even waiting for a reply, added: 'Why didn't you tell me? I read about it on the internet! Get us a backstage pass, Bela.'

'Well, it's a bit late in the da–'

That wasn't good enough for Priyanka, who quickly interrupted Bela. *'Pleeeeeeaaaasse!* I'll be there cheering you on. You need at least one fan there, don't you?' she joked.

'Very funny,' Bela replied.

'And I promise I won't embarrass you like Tara did with the VideoWeb stuff – even though I think the mad cow's the funniest thing ever.'

'If I do get you in, you'd better not do anything to show me up, Priyanka,' said Bela firmly. 'Tara was funny but she's kind of made this Monica situation worse for me. Some people are so thick they think I was laughing at Monica, even though it's obvious I'm only laughing at Tara's impression. Anyway, I know why you really want to go. It's just to ogle Marc and the other actors, isn't it?'

'Oh, please Bela. I don't get to go anywhere – especially not glitzy, glamorous places like this!'

'Mmm. Okay, I'll see what I can do,' said Bela, realising her friend would be quite upset if she didn't at least make an effort for her. 'I'll try to sort you out. I'll call my agent and see if she can organise it. But if you do get in, don't go acting like a mushy teenager, drooling over all the stars. They're ordinary people like you and me, so just act cool, yeah?'

'Anything you say, matey. See you later,' said Priyanka, very hopefully.

True to her word, Bela called Jaya to organise Priyanka's pass, and then plonked herself down on the plush turquoise sofa in the family's living room. She tried to relax, but she couldn't help thinking about the evening ahead. Bela had only been acting for a year-and-a-half and to get two nominations was a massive achievement. She was up for the Best Actress award for *Maid in India* and Best Supporting Actress award for *Kismet*.

'I'm so looking forward to this evening,' beamed Bela's mum, as she entered the living room with two cups of tea. She sat down next to Bela. 'You know, your father and I are very proud of you. You've come such a long way, and you've done such a lot for the family. If it wasn't for you, we would never be sitting here,' she stated, looking straight out through the huge glass doors in front of her and marvelling at the fabulous views of the Arabian Sea.

It was raining hard, but it made the view even more spectacular as the waves crashed mercilessly against the rocks.

Bela had bought the luxurious beachside villa after the release of her second movie, *Maid in India*, which was a runaway success, just like her debut film, *Pyar Hua*. It was in the most elegant part of Mumbai and Bela loved the fact that you could glimpse the historical Gateway of India from her bedroom window.

'If you win an award, I'll jump up and down like a maniac,' her mum suddenly burst out. She put her arm around Bela and gave her a very tight squeeze.

'Mind my tea, Mum!'

'Oh, sorry darling,' she continued, releasing Bela from her grasp. 'I can't help being so excited. It'll be unbelievable if you win. And you know what? I think you're in with a good chance – unless Monica does something sneaky, of course.'

'Oh Mum,' said Bela, shaking her head. 'Trust you to ruin this lovely relaxing moment by bringing her up. Honestly!'

'Sorry, Baby, but someone's got to say it, haven't

they? She's a sly little thing who thinks she owns Bollywood, but she needs to be told – if there is a queen of Bollywood, it's you. It's Bela!'

Bela chuckled. Her mum was so dramatic and Bela and Reuben were convinced it was because she'd watched far too many Indian movies.

'Anyway,' said Bela, after a moment's pause, 'this function isn't being organised by Monica's dad or his mates. The filmgoers decide who the winners are. Well, that's what *FilmGlitz* claims anyway,' she added as the doorbell chimed. 'I'll get it. It's probably Micky. We've got less than two hours to get ready.'

Bela opened the door and wanted to explode with laughter at the sight that greeted her. Standing on the doorstep was one very wet, bedraggled-looking woman. It was Mili, her hairdresser.

Mili, also known as Mad Mili because of her high-pitched laugh, was completely drenched. She was a short, well-rounded woman and was wearing beige jeans that were so wet they clung to her like a second skin. She had no coat or umbrella, just an equally wet, black shawl draped over her shoulders and head.

'Oh, Mili!' sympathised Bela. 'Come in. How did you manage to get so wet? I could have got Raju to pick you up.'

'I would have called you if I'd known I was gonna end up like this. My car broke down,' she began as she removed her shawl. Mili loved telling stories, even if they were about nothing.

'So I had to get a cab,' she continued. 'Then, halfway into the journey, I realised the driver was the same guy who ripped me off last week when I was coming back from a magazine shoot, so I started arguing with him. Then he stopped the taxi, said I was accusing him of being dishonest, and abandoned me. Can you believe it?' she went on.

'I had to walk, but he didn't get paid, so at least I saved 160 rupees. Do you think this soaking is worth 160 rupees?' Mili asked, glancing over at Bela, who by now didn't know whether to laugh at Mili's tale or cry because she was wasting so much time.

Thankfully, Bela's mum cut in. 'Come on, Mili. I'll give you some dry clothes and you can tell us your story over a cup of tea – but only after you've started on Bela's hair. We don't have much time!'

'Oh, yes, Bela's hair. Come on, dear, what are you waiting for?' said Mili, as though Bela was holding her up. 'You heard your ma, we're running out of time and you have to look a million dollars as you are the Bela of the ball,' she laughed. 'Bela of the ball! Ha ha! Geddit, geddit?' She cackled hysterically.

Mother and daughter were vaguely amused but, realising they had no time for jokes, decided not to encourage her. Mili got to work and as she started putting rollers into Bela's hair, Micky arrived with his make-up kit along with Manju, Bela's newly-appointed wardrobe manager.

'Oh my!' exclaimed Bela, her eyes lighting up. She was over the moon to see Manju turn up with the most gorgeous pale blue chiffon saree with pearl-white embroidery. 'That is the most amazing saree I have ever seen – so '60s but so "now". Thanks, Manju, thank you!' she beamed, giving her a big warm hug.

'Wow! That is a stunner,' added Mili as she clapped her eyes on the outfit. 'Micky, Mili and Manju. Perhaps we should form a partnership, a new business and call it 'Mmm'. That's a great idea. Geddit, M-M-M... Mmm... Our initials... *ha ha ha ha ha*!' She was in hysterics again, and this time no-one in the room could help but giggle along with this fabulous hairdresser with the fabulously corny sense of humour.

Bela smiled to herself. She loved being pampered and she loved dressing up. She felt she'd had a bit of a rough time lately, but now things were going well. Bela felt totally content as Team Mmm got to work, every member with the sole aim of making her look gorgeous.

Sixty minutes later, expertly draped in the saree with matching accessories and high heels, and her hair in an elaborate up-do, Bela looked every inch the movie star.

Chapter 4

As Bela stepped daintily out of her big stretch limousine, putting her pretty, painted feet on to the red carpet, everyone clamoured to catch a glimpse of her. Cameras flashed and she waved at everyone with the confidence and poise expected of a superstar.

On the inside though, her heart was racing. Bela was touched by the response she was receiving now, and even though she was very keen to perform on stage with Marc, she felt nervous about the awards.

'Bela, Bela, please look this way,' shouted the photographers eagerly. The crowd was cheering like mad.

She stopped to look around at all the people who were so kindly showing their appreciation for her. It was almost surreal. She still found it hard to believe that just eighteen months ago she had been an ordinary schoolgirl, and today she was like royalty.

Thankfully for everyone who had turned out, the heavy rain had finally stopped and instead it was showering superstars. One by one, the biggest names in the film business pulled up outside the Royal Theatre Hall. Shantripriya, Ajit Bedi, Shahbaaz Khan, Marc Fernandez, Ajay Banerjee and Raakhee Supriyo were just some of the famous faces to show up and the fans loved every minute of it.

People were jammed into every nook and cranny of the street, virtually jumping over each other for a glimpse of their celluloid heroes. As for the press, now that Bela had made her appearance, their eyes were peeled for Monica. They needed good headlines and she was sure to provide them.

Bela was doing her final round of interviews outside the theatre, relieved that nobody had yet brought up Tara's VideoWeb sketches, when Monica's pink Cadillac pulled up. There were only ten minutes left before the show began, which meant that Monica wouldn't have time for interviews. She was slightly less organised than Bela, but a bit more PR-savvy, and she believed in being fashionably late.

'The more you keep people waiting, the more they want to see you,' Monica whispered to her dad as she got out of the car.

'That's my girl!' he laughed, patting her on the back. Monica stretched up and stood tall. She was wearing a silver-grey, full-length silk dress that was slashed at her right leg, all the way up to her thigh.

The snappers got really excited.

'Show us your lovely legs!' yelled one. 'It'll be front page news.'

Monica preened herself and struck a few sultry poses for the eager cameramen. 'More! More!' shouted another.

'Give us another pose,' screamed a third.

This was the reaction she'd hoped for. All was going to plan. Monica posed expertly and flashed that famous, big white smile of hers. She was wearing a stunning necklace set with huge diamonds and matching bracelet that twinkled brightly against the backdrop of the dark sky.

Bela, who was stood just a few feet away doing a TV interview, was aware of the commotion Monica was causing but chose not to look in her direction. With all these journalists around, she thought they may be looking for some kind of reaction from her.

Monica continued to bask in all the attention until one person broke in with a question that changed her entire mood. 'Looking forward to the head-to-head with Bela over the Best Actress award?' he bellowed from the crowd somewhere. 'Or are you smiling 'cos you know you've already won? A case of "Dad'll Fix It"!'

There were roars of laughter.

Monica's eyes darted around as she tried to find out who had the nerve to be so rude. As his fellow reporters mischievously pointed him out, she looked at the culprit with her piercing black eyes, grabbed Papa, who was waiting by the sidelines, by the arm and disappeared inside.

* * *

The atmosphere inside the Royal Theatre Hall was magical. There were huge plasma screens dotted around the place, flashing up images of all the most famous movie stars in Bollywood's history and so many bright, twinkly lights everywhere it was like Diwali.

Nobody wanted to miss out on such a prestigious function and Bela was impressed to see that all the biggest names in the film industry had turned up. In fact, it was like a Who's Who of Bollywood, past and present. She was honoured to be a part of this glitzy affair, but was also beginning to feel the nerves again as she settled down at one of the main tables alongside her parents and other chief guests.

The winners were selected by a public poll, and even though she knew the outcome didn't really matter in the big scheme of things, her confidence would naturally be boosted by a win and slightly dampened if she didn't go home with a trophy. She hoped it didn't show on her face, but her stomach was doing somersaults.

'It's the taking part that counts,' said Shammi Ahmed, a veteran film director seated at the same table. He hungrily tucked into the starters that the waiters had dished out.

'Of course you're in with a great chance, but even if you don't win, Bela, the fact that you've been nominated at the age of sixteen is a huge accomplishment. I didn't get a nomination until I was 35, and even then I went home empty-handed. Oh yes, I remember it well,' he reminisced with a faraway look in his eyes.

Bela smiled sweetly and nodded, as though she agreed. She was touched that Shammi*ji* spoke so highly of her achievements but she couldn't get herself to say that the awards didn't matter, because she suddenly found herself wanting to win. *Really badly.* In the presence of all these legendary names, at this moment in time, she felt as though her life depended on it.

Of course, it was the Best Actress award that mattered most to Bela. It was the more prestigious prize, but also it was this category in which she was up against Monica, who was seated two tables away, to Bela's right.

Aware that people could be watching to see if Bela was checking out the competition, she made a point of not doing so. But there was another reason she didn't want to look over to Monica's table. Shashi Kumar had already cut a few glances in Bela's direction and he didn't look too happy. Had he also seen Tara's impression of his daughter? If he had, Bela was sure that he would see Bela's laughing as bitchy. Bela tried to imagine how she would have felt if Monica had been laughing at an imitation of her. Not so good, she was sure.

Bela's mum, on the other hand, had no such feelings. 'You look miles better than Monica,' she whispered to Bela.

'Keep your voice down, Mum.'

'Okay, her jewels are quite sparkly, but who knows if they're real? They must be fake – nobody can have that many diamonds!'

'How do you know?' asked Bela.

'Trust me, I know. And look at the colour of her dress! She looks drab in grey. Your saree, your hair, your jewellery… everything is so much better. Your look is a real showstealer.'

'Shhh, Mum,' urged Bela, nudging her very slightly with her elbow. 'Don't stare at her! You're gonna make the whole thing even worse, if that's possible. And no, I don't think I look better than her. She looks great, okay? Dad! Keep Ma under control, please!'

Her dad, Krishan, laughed. He thought the whole thing was hilarious. 'Yes, of course, dear. But please tell me that I look more dapper than Monica's dad,' he added, straightening his tie. 'It's important that *we* look better than *them*.'

Bela fired a stern look straight at her father. She knew it was his idea of a joke, but she couldn't see the funny side of it right now. It was definitely the wrong place at the wrong time. Both her parents were giggling like a pair of teenagers and Bela wondered if it had been such a good idea to bring them along.

'If Reuben was in town, I would have brought him with me and left both of you at home,' she remarked, turning her face slightly so the other people seated at the table couldn't tell she was reprimanding her mum and dad. 'Now I know why Reuben never takes you two anywhere.' She folded her arms and tightened up.

Realising they had gone a bit too far, her parents stopped laughing and turned to look at the stage instead. The soft instrumental music playing in the background gave way to a thumping upbeat tune as the main function got underway.

As anticipated, the opening act was spectacular. Scores of brightly-dressed dancers burst on to the stage and wowed the crowd with their contemporary Indian dance. The performers were beautifully synchronised and the dancing set the tone perfectly for the rest of the evening.

The piece was very entertaining and well-rehearsed, Bela thought. She knew that both she and Marc had a high standard to live up to, but they had performed their dance quite recently at a local charity function and she felt confident they wouldn't let the side down.

After two hours of singing, dancing, special appearances by film stars of years gone by and announcements of winners in a whole gamut of categories from editing to choreography, it was finally time for the result of the Best Supporting Actress award.

On the surface, Bela looked completely composed, but inside she was suddenly wishing for the night to be over so she could stop feeling like a wobbly jelly.

'And the winner is...' announced the glamorous veteran actress Sheila Batra, opening the golden envelope. 'Pooja Bhaskar for *Dil!*'

The hall erupted in applause for young Pooja, who had made her impressive debut in this film. Bela's mum frowned, but Bela and her dad applauded Pooja. Strangely, Bela didn't feel bad about losing out to Pooja as she really admired her work in the film. And if the cameras zoomed in on her, at least it wouldn't look as though she was jealous of her pretty colleague's success.

'Phew!' Bela gasped a few minutes later when the attention had moved away from her again. 'One down, one to go. Oh dear, Dad, this night isn't going the way I imagined it would at all. I thought it was gonna be fun, but I'm a bag of nerves and I have to look as though I'm having a great time! I almost wish I'd never been nominated. At least I could have enjoyed the show that way.'

Her dad smiled. 'You young girls take everything so seriously. Relax, it's only an awards night, there'll be hundreds of these in your career – touch wood! Get used to them, girl.'

'I don't know how you can sit there so happily

and calmly, Krishan,' said Bela's mum, annoyed with him for not being upset, angry or nervous. 'Forget how Bela's feeling – I'm a complete mess too! Get me a drink, please!'

'No way, Mum!' said Bela, looking horrified. 'You are *not* drinking. Even one glass makes you go crazy, so please, not here. Gosh, I need a distraction from you two. Have you spotted Priyanka anywhere, Dad? I'm sure Jaya must have got her a pass to get in but I haven't seen her.'

He shook his head, poured himself another glass of sparkling mineral water and then turned to Shammi Ahmed to talk about the lack of good golfing facilities in India. Bela's mum tutted loudly as she realised the direction the conversation was taking and was just about to interrupt, but she was soon distracted. The results of the Best Actress award were about to be announced.

Bela was feeling even more pressure this time. What if the audience preferred Monica to her? She had a serious case of butterflies.

'Smile, Bela,' nudged her mum as she sipped orange juice, her hands trembling slightly. 'All eyes are on you now. If you lose, be gracious. Just smile crazily either way!'

'I'm trying,' said Bela, smiling and nodding her

head cheerfully. 'Believe me, I'm trying!'

The show was being hosted by comedian Jimmy Contractor and now his voice boomed across the magnificent hall. 'Nominations for the *FilmGlitz* Magazine Best Actress of the year are... Rani Mahalaxmi for *Raja Rani*, Bela for *Maid in India*, Monica for *Taj Mahal* and Sharmila Dhillon for *Call Centre*.'

Ageing superstar Deepak Rana, once adored for his rippling muscles and devilish good looks but now more admired for his acting skills, lifted the golden envelope and Bela closed her eyes.

Everyone seated at Monica's table began chanting 'Mon-i-ca! Mon-i-ca!' and she sat beaming with confidence.

'Well, she's either supremely confident or she's a better actress than I thought,' commented Bela's mum. 'It's as though she knows she's won it!'

Bela sneaked a glance at Monica and her group. Seeing how upbeat and self-assured they all looked, Bela was suddenly certain she hadn't won. Nevertheless, she strained to be positive, and reminded herself how lucky she was to be nominated at all. At least her butterflies had gone.

Bela peered up at the giant screen that was showing film clips of the nominated actresses in action and waited for Monica's name to be announced as winner.

'All stunning aren't they?' winked Deepak once the screen had gone blank. The audience whistled and cheered in agreement. 'Here we go. The winner of the Best Actress Award is… the beautiful… Bel-aaaaaaaaaaaaaaaaaa!'

'Oh my God!' Bela shrieked. She was so stunned that she clapped a hand to her mouth as her jaw dropped. Her heart was racing and her legs were trembling. She wasn't sure that she'd be able to stand, let alone walk up to the stage to collect her trophy.

Thankfully, she was helped to her feet by her overjoyed mum who was throwing flying kisses at the cameras zooming in on the family.

Bela was swamped by different emotions – joy at winning the award, nervousness at going up to collect it and embarrassment by her mum's over-the-top reaction. In spite of it all, though, Bela noticed that the mood at Monica's table was markedly different. The ten members of her party were very quiet and made no effort to applaud Bela at all.

Bela caught a brief glimpse of Monica being sympathy-hugged by her dad as she weaved her way gracefully to the stage, but she didn't dare look directly at them. She wanted nothing to take away her enjoyment of this moment, especially not Monica. She truly felt as though she was on top of the world.

Beaming, she accepted the award from Deepak, who had been her childhood hero, and gave him a hug. She was surprised to find that close up he was not at all as she had imagined, or remembered. He looked much shorter than he appeared on screen and he had definitely lost the fresh-faced appeal that had catapulted him to fame and made him the darling of millions around the world.

'So, beautiful Bela, I bet you're thrilled to win this prestigious honour,' he said, looking admiringly at her. Then, out of the blue, he added, 'Is your impersonator friend here, because I feel she deserves the comic award of the year? No offence, Monica!'

The audience exploded with laughter and Bela felt her face flush red. Fortunately, Deepak moved swiftly on.

'And I have another surprise for you today, young lady,' he said cheerily. 'Perhaps you didn't know this, but you are the youngest person to ever win a *FilmGlitz* Best Actress Award. No doubt that makes it even more special. Ladies and Gentlemen, please put your hands together for Bela – a star at sweet sixteen!'

The audience clapped as Deepak handed Bela the microphone so she could say a few words to the gathered onlookers and all those watching the show on satellite TV around the world.

'I'm shocked but so… so delighted to receive this trophy,' she began, nervously. 'Everyone nominated is a fantastic actress, so it's an incredible honour to find out the public thinks I am the best!' Bela smiled, looking radiant with happiness.

'And I'm even more thrilled to be the youngest-ever recipient of this award. I'd like to thank my family, friends and fans for their support over the past year and also everyone who was involved in *Maid in India*, from spot boys and assistants to the director. It was a really great experience. I'd also like to congratulate the other girls for their brilliant work in the movies they were nominated for.'

She didn't manage to say much more than that. Bela was too overwhelmed to be able to think clearly and was just glad she hadn't burst into tears like so many of the Hollywood starlets did.

Bela descended the stairs to make her way back to her table and loud cheers resonated through the hall for her. But as she was coming back down to earth, she couldn't help noticing that something was missing.

It was Monica.

Chapter 5

The next morning Bela had a well-deserved lie-in. She didn't open her eyes until ten and the first thing she did was look around the room for her award. It still felt as though it might all have been a dream.

'It's real, all right,' she said, grinning to herself as

she looked lovingly at the red figurine sitting in pride of place on her dressing table. But she pinched herself as well just to make sure once and for all that this really, really was happening, and once she caught a glimpse of Priyanka tucked up and snoring away at the foot-end of her bed, she was satisfied that this wasn't some crazy, far-fetched dream.

Bela lay back down again and replayed the events of the previous night in her mind. Even though her body ached from her energetic dance performance with Marc at the end of the night, and she had blisters on her feet from the ill-fitting shoes she'd worn, she felt great. Marc had looked genuinely happy that she had won an award and he'd given her a warm, lingering hug backstage before their dance together. And that's also where she'd found Priyanka.

Priyanka wasn't as crazy or daring as Tara, but she was just as star-struck and wanted to make full use of her backstage privileges. She didn't quite conjure up the courage to talk to any of the actors or actresses, but she stood gawping shamelessly at every one she spotted.

'Priyanka, Priyanka, wake up,' whispered Bela, gently tugging at the far end of her duvet. 'Look, my award… I can't believe I won!'

There was no response – Priyanka was dead to

the world. And it wasn't surprising, considering the girls and Bela's parents hadn't got home until four in the morning. This was partly because of the time it took for Bela to chat to all the TV and press reporters eager to talk to her, and also because Bela and Priyanka then insisted on going to the after-show party at a nightclub called Tiger's Pause.

Priyanka had wanted to rub shoulders with celebrities for even longer and Bela was feeling so good she wanted the evening to go on and on. They all boogied the night away until three thirty and it was only when Bela's dad begged the girls to spare his 50-year-old body that they decided to call it a night.

'Wake up, girls,' shouted Bela's mum from the bottom of the stairs. 'Priyanka's mum just called to say she's gonna be over to pick her up in a little while. It's gone ten o'clock and your breakfast is ready – scrambled eggs and beans. Oh – and Bela, the Sunday papers are here.'

Bela jumped out of bed, threw her dressing gown on and ran downstairs. She couldn't wait to see the papers with all their photos and write-ups from the night before. Bela knew she had been the star of the show and she was sure to be in all the headlines.

She was right about making it into the papers.

But as she glanced over the headlines of *The Sunday Herald's* entertainment section, Bela quickly realised this thrill was going to be short-lived. The main headline ran: 'VICTORY FOR BELA WHO DECLARES: "I AM A BETTER ACTRESS THAN MONICA".'

She couldn't believe her eyes. How had Monica's name even made it into the same headline? It seemed impossible. The whole evening had gone by without incident as far as she was concerned. Monica hadn't hung around long enough to cause controversy. Bela was truly stunned.

'Mum, have you read this?'

'What's that, Baby?' asked her mum, taking the paper out of Bela's hands and holding it at arm's length so her longsighted eyes could focus. She began reading: 'Victory for Bela who declares I am a better actress than Monica.'

'What the hell has Monica got to do with this?' Bela asked angrily before her mum had even had a chance to comment. 'It's not fair! I thought there would be some good, honest reporting for a change...' Her voice trailed off.

Bela's mum sat down to think. It was a rare thing indeed to see this vociferous woman lost for words, but Sheila didn't know what to say either. Bela was sure this was partly because her mum was suffering from a hangover. She was sitting holding one side of her head, obviously paying the price for defying Bela's orders at the awards after-party and treating herself to not one, but three glasses of champagne.

Bela's mum saw how upset she was and realised that being negative wouldn't help. She would have to play her own feelings down.

'Oh dear,' she began, putting the paper to one side and walking over to where Bela was standing with her arms folded.

Bela was facing the glass doors that looked out to the sea. Sheila put her arm gently around her daughter's shoulder and gave her a little squeeze.

'Don't let it upset you Bela. The newspapers just need to sell copies. It's the way of the world. Sadly, they feel this will help them sell more.'

She continued, 'I guess it's not their fault – I remember buying copies of *FilmGlitz* magazine years ago to read about the rivalries between top stars of my generation. Looking back now, I'm sure many of those stories were made up too.'

Sheila screwed up her face, looking annoyed as it dawned on her that she'd been cheated. 'Gosh, and to think I used to save my pocket money to buy them and then read every word and take it as gospel.

That's absolutely terrible!'

'But it is NOT FAIR!' shrieked Bela, in a manner most unlike her. She was normally so softly-spoken that to hear her shout or even speak loudly was very unusual. In fact, it even woke Priyanka, who rushed downstairs to see what the commotion was all about.

'I did not *say* or *mean* that!' continued Bela, getting more wound-up by the second.

'I know that, Baby.'

'Mum, I chose the words in my speech very carefully precisely because I didn't want to upset anyone. I said "I'm glad the audience thinks I'm better" or something like that. I can't even remember the exact words. And I made a point of congratulating the other heroines, but – surprise, surprise – there's no mention of that!'

'She's right,' added Priyanka, even though she didn't quite know what the fuss was all about. 'I saw Bela's speech on the big TV screen backstage. I was watching Marc rehearse. I think he was just about to come over and speak to me when his phone rang.'

Bela cut a look at Priyanka as if to say 'now is not the time' and Priyanka took the hint, speedily leaving the room. As Priyanka went upstairs to get dressed, Bela's dad walked in through the front door with a pair of golf clubs in his hand. For somebody who had claimed to be 'all done in' a few hours before, he seemed to have made a rather wonderful recovery, thought Bela. He was as sprightly as ever and didn't look as though he'd had a late night.

'Has anyone seen my other clubs?' he asked, totally oblivious to the enormity of the situation brewing in his living room.

'Dad, have you seen this?'

'What, darling? Oh that, yes,' he replied. 'Just now, as I was leaving the golf club. I thought it was a bit inaccurate – I'm sure you didn't say that. But it doesn't really matter, does it?'

'What?' asked Bela in disbelief. 'What do you mean it doesn't matter?'

'Well, no publicity is bad publicity at the end of the day,' he said, and continued, 'You may think this is a bad way to get column inches, but it does mean that people will read about you. And the more they read, the more journalists will write about you, so the more popular you'll become and the more films you'll be offered. Simple. It's all about column inches. Just watch how much mileage you and Monica get out of this – not that either of you needs it, of course.'

'See Baby,' Sheila piped up. 'Your Dad's right. Maybe it's a good thing after all.'

'Mum! Dad!' Bela yelled, stomping her foot on the floor in sheer annoyance. 'I don't care about stupid column inches! I don't want untrue things written about me and I don't want people to think I've made these pompous claims when I haven't. I don't care about the publicity, but I do care about my reputation and what my fans think of me!'

'And from today, you will have twice as many fans. Guaranteed!' added Krishan chirpily, bending down to see if his clubs were hiding under the sofa.

'Aha, here they are. We're gonna thrash the Patels today, aren't we, boys?' he said, talking to the golf clubs as though they could hear him. Then he bounced back up and brushed the dust from his knees.

'Oh, what's the point? You care more about your golf than how I feel!' Bela snapped in frustration. She grabbed the newspapers, dumped them in the corner of the room and stormed off upstairs to see if Priyanka would side with her on this one.

'Oh, Priyanka,' said Bela, distraught. She shut the bedroom door behind her and went and sat on her bed.

'This is all so stressful. I hate being in any kind of controversy and now all this stuff has been splashed over the papers about me saying I'm better than

Monica and the whole world is gonna think I'm arrogant and full of myself and they'll all hate me,' she spat out in one long breath. 'I wish we were still in school – we had no worries back then.'

Priyanka, who was struggling to zip her boots up over her chunky calves, looked up and gave Bela a disbelieving stare. 'That's what you were making a fuss about downstairs?' she asked.

'Yeah.'

'I thought something really bad had happened the way you were going on, but it was just the papers? So let's get this straight – you're annoyed because the press quoted you as saying something about Monica that you didn't really say?'

Bela nodded.

'And that's it?' continued Priyanka, probing her friend.

'Well, yeah. I guess so,' replied Bela. 'That's it. But it's terrible – people will think I'm a big-headed cow and that I think I'm a better actress than Monica.'

'Okay, so who is the better actress – you or Monica?'

Bela sat down to think before giving her final answer. 'I guess I am. Monica's okay, but I don't think she can do the full range of roles like I can.

I'm not being big-headed, just honest.'

'Right,' said Priyanka. 'So the papers aren't actually wrong, are they? Which means you've got nothing to worry about.'

Bela went quiet.

'*You*, girlfriend, need your head examined!' said Priyanka, pointing at Bela and raising her voice at the same time. '*You* hated school, *we* hated school. And now you have this amazing life and you're worried about a tiny thing like a newspaper article, which doesn't even say anything untrue. You should just feel glad they consider you important enough to write about in the first place!'

All of a sudden, Bela started feeling a bit foolish. She could see where this conversation was heading and didn't really want to hear any more. But she let Priyanka have her say because Bela felt she probably deserved it, and perhaps even needed to hear it.

'I would die to be in your shoes, you wally,' Priyanka continued. 'I would die to be in all the magazines, but who wants to read about me? I've just left school, I'm training as a beautician and that's it. Hardly hot news. Give me glamour, fancy outfits, movies, travel and Marc Fernandez any day. I'll take all the gossip the mags can churn out.'

Bela didn't say a thing. She just smiled. Her very

simple, straightforward schoolfriend had just turned her mountain into a molehill and she was extremely grateful for that.

chapter 6

Priyanka and Bela stayed upstairs for a while and had a long chat about everything.

They talked about the time when Bela's mum came bursting into the classroom with a pair of shoes because she'd sent Bela to school in her flip-flops, and the time that Priyanka got detention for charging money to paint her friends' nails during break times. They had a good chuckle, and Bela was glad to be able to laugh freely and not worry about who was watching, what Monica was up to, or what Shashi Kumar and the rest of the world thought of her.

Sadly, the time spent reminiscing with Priyanka flew by, and before she knew it Priyanka's mum was at the door waiting to pick her daughter up.

'Well done on the award, Bela!' congratulated Priyanka's mum, pinching Bela's cheek really hard as though she was still nine years old. She had a shrill, rather irritating voice. 'Get my girl into the movies too and you can both work together!'

Sheila immediately looked over at Bela and tried to catch her eye. Bela knew her mum thought that was highly unlikely, but she avoided her gaze, not wanting Priyanka or her mother to pick up on this. Instead, Bela gave Priyanka a warm hug and thanked her for helping her celebrate her award victory, as well as for the much-needed pep talk.

Once Priyanka had gone, Bela felt she should try to hang out with her parents for a while, realising she'd been a bit unreasonable to take her frustrations with the media out on them. And now that Priyanka had helped her put the whole issue into perspective, she agreed it wasn't that much of a big deal.

'Where's Dad?' asked Bela, following her mum into the living room.

'Gone golfing, as usual.'

'Oh, that's a shame. I thought we could all go out or do something together,' said Bela.

'Well, that's a nice thought – and it's good to see you looking a bit chirpier,' said Sheila as she tidied up the living room, which was looking a real state.

'Yeah, it's not the end of the world,' remarked Bela, removing her sparkly hair grip and tying a knot in her long hair to make a simple bun. 'I've got to stop letting this kind of stuff get to me or I'll turn into a screaming lunatic. How about we forget about the stupid papers and do something that has nothing to do with films today?'

'That's a great idea, Bela,' replied her mum, clicking her fingers in readiness. 'How about–'

Bela didn't even let her mum finish. 'No, no studying today, please! I'm knackered. I'll catch up over the next few days.' She shook her head in despair – she knew what was going to come next.

Her distance-learning Information Technology course was a regular cause of dispute in the house and now that her mum had started, she wasn't going to let it drop easily.

'You promised us you'd devote a bit more time to your studies if we let you work in movies full-time,' reminded her mum. 'This is why your dad and I wanted you to stay at school – we knew this was going to happen.' Sheila folded her arms and looked very cross.

Bela understood why her mum and dad had wanted her to stay on at school, but she'd quit as soon as she'd turned sixteen. Bela had been signed up for her first movie at the age of fourteen, and for more than a year was studying and filming side by side. Once her debut movie went on to become a blockbuster, though, Bela was inundated with offers and wanted to do what she loved on a full-time basis.

'Look, Mum, I know I need something to fall back on and I will complete the course, but there's no deadline or hurry and I'm allowed to take as long as I like. I have to fit it in around my work, and right now I'm tired.'

'You've been saying that for weeks now,' her mum moaned. 'Your two-year course will take nine years at this rate.'

Bela tutted loudly. Her mum had a habit of exaggerating everything.

'So what if it takes nine years?' Bela challenged.

'I can finish it when I'm 50 years old if I want. But who's gonna give me lead roles as a heroine at 50? Nobody.'

Sheila looked at Bela and fell silent for a brief moment, realising her daughter had a point. 'Look, I love movies too, but education is important,' she tried to explain as calmly as possible.

'And you need to understand that you're lucky we allowed you into the business at all. Your grandparents are still angry with us for letting you become a film star in the first place. They think that all actresses are… umm… how can I put this? They think all actresses are of ill-repute.'

Bela shook her head. She'd heard all this before, but she knew she had to let her mother get it off her chest. Sheila went through this routine on a regular basis. She'd go on a rant about Bela's education, then forget about it for a while and be really proud of her daughter, the movie star. Then something would spark her off and the cycle would start again. Today was definitely a rant day.

'Education comes first, films after,' her mum jabbered on as she polished the marble coffee table. 'We're not a cheap *filmi* family like that Monica girl's. We are respectable people.'

Bela yawned and, before her mum could say

anything else, walked out of the room to call her agent.

'I don't want to take any calls today, Jaya,' Bela informed her, feeling too drained by the morning's events to exchange pleasantries. 'Yes… I know about the papers. Everyone knows. But it's not my fault and I'm not really in the mood to talk about it. We'll speak tomorrow. Bye.'

She sent Reuben a text message to fill him in on the latest happenings in Tinsel Town and their mother's education crusade, then switched her mobile phone off and chucked it into the kitchen drawer. She strode decisively back into the living room, grabbed all the offending newspapers and dumped them into the rubbish bin.

'There!' she exclaimed, wiping her hands as though the content of the newspapers had somehow soiled them. 'That's what I think of all that so-called journalism. And now for my next trick, Mum – I'm going to amaze you – I think it may be time for that long overdue clearout.'

'My, my!' exclaimed Sheila, raising a hand to her mouth in genuine shock. 'So it takes a major PR disaster to get you to sort your clothes out. Hurrah for bad press!'

Mother and daughter both smiled. Bela was glad

that she'd decided not to waste any more time dwelling on silly newspaper headlines and focus on pleasing her mum instead. Besides, this was the best way to divert the topic away from the great education debate.

The pair decided to begin Project Clearout in Bela's bedroom by getting rid of all the clothes that she no longer wore – and some she had never worn at all. There were plenty of them. As a sought-after star, Bela was constantly being given freebies by top designers eager for her to model their creations.

'Gosh, do you remember how I used to wear the same clothes over and over again until they had holes in?' Bela chuckled, as she pulled out a bunch of dresses from her wardrobe.

''Course I do,' replied her mum. 'It wasn't that long ago! You'd have holes in your jeans and be begging me to patch them up. Now you get all these things for free and you don't even get round to wearing half of them.'

'Well, some of them are *definitely* not my style,' said Bela, holding up a bright green satin dress with garish pink embroidery. 'I'll put these aside – Tara and Priyanka might like them. If not, we'll give them to charity.'

As they busily made up tidy little piles, the

doorbell rang. 'I'll get it,' said Bela, jumping up. 'Can you please put the stuff we've selected for the girls by the side of the bed? I'll invite them round later in the week.'

She skipped off downstairs to open the front door and was taken aback to be greeted by a massive bouquet of exotic orange and pink flowers.

Bela looked quizzically at the FloralWorld delivery man who had been let in through the main gates by the security guard. He was holding up a piece of paper for her to sign and just shrugged his shoulders to indicate he didn't know who the flowers were from. He then just grinned at her, obviously dumbstruck to see such a huge film star on his daily round.

Once she'd parted with two signatures – one for the flowers and one in the form of an autograph for the overjoyed messenger – Bela took the bunch into the kitchen to put them in a vase.

'But who are they from? They're not from Reuben, that's definitely not his style,' she muttered to herself as she dug around in the bunch looking for a note. 'They're not from Marc, are they?' she suddenly thought. Her heart skipped a beat. Bela pulled the small envelope out, held her breath and opened it.

The message read: '*Congrats on the award. Want to be in Om Shankara's next movie? Meet with producers today, Kohinoor Hotel, 5pm.*'

Bela just stared at it for a while, not knowing what to make of it. It was an odd way to get a film offer, but Om Shankara…

'MUM!' she yelled, plonking the flowers on the worktop and leaping up the stairs with the piece of paper in her hand. 'Look!'

Her mum looked at the note and read it twice to make sure she hadn't misinterpreted anything – her head was still fuzzy from the night before. 'Hmm, it's a bit strange that they haven't approached Jaya… but then again, maybe they wanted to grab your attention. Or perhaps they're in a hurry.'

'Oh my God!' said Bela, eyes lighting up. 'Do you really think that Om Shankara is in a hurry to cast his next movie?'

'It's possible.'

'Maybe they want to make a decision today,' Bela suddenly thought. 'Oh, wow! Actresses are falling over themselves to work with him. He's the best! You wouldn't believe the things people do just to get him to consider them for his films – it's shocking. But he wants me!' Bela was thrilled, and clutched the note tightly to her chest.

'Well, you're the best actress in town, why wouldn't he want you?' asked Sheila.

'Maybe Dad's right, perhaps this is because of all the publicity! Gosh, I don't know what to do. It's gone three o'clock already. I'd better get dressed – I don't know where to start,' she said, raising her hands to her head and feeling flustered. 'Sorry about the clearout, Mum, it'll have to wait.'

'Hmmm, I thought it was too good to be true,' Sheila replied, as she picked up the piles of clothes that were dotted around Bela's room. 'I guess we'll just have to do it another day. Off you go then, go and get ready,' she said, secretly glad that they didn't have to make up any more piles. All she wanted to do was put her head down and sleep.

Bela tried to call Jaya to see if she'd come to the meeting with her, but there was no reply on her landline and her mobile was switched off. She thought about passing by Jaya's house on the way, but she lived on the outskirts of Mumbai and the hotel was in the centre so there wasn't enough time.

For a moment Bela even contemplated taking her mum with her, but remembering her rather cringe-worthy performance from the night before she quickly pushed that thought to the most distant corner of her mind.

No, she would have to go to the Kohinoor Hotel alone. Bela called Raju to make sure he could take her, and within thirty minutes she had showered and was dressed in a pair of trendy white jeans and an olive roll-neck pullover, topped off with a smart white jacket. Looking in her full-length mirror to assess the final result, Bela was pleased to discover she looked very presentable in a casual kind of way.

'Raju will drive me there. I'll be back soon, Mum,' she said, giving her a peck on the cheek.

'Good luck, Baby. Be back by dinner. And don't sign anything until you've spoken to Jaya! We pay her for a reason – there are some real sharks out there. Maybe I should go with you…'

Bela sensed it was time to make a dash for the door. 'No, no, you rest. Don't worry. I won't sign anything, but perhaps there'll be reason for a glass – or three – of champagne tonight!'

'Oh, stop!' Sheila groaned. 'Just the thought of it is making my head spin. See you later.'

It was a Sunday, so there was less traffic than usual and Bela reached the luxurious hotel at a quarter to five. The Kohinoor in Mumbai was one of the most famous five-star hotels in the country. It was more than one hundred years old and it just seemed to ooze history.

Bela looked up at the sprawling marble building as she stepped out of the car and admired its magnificent architecture.

'Good, I'm fifteen minutes early – I don't want to look unprofessional,' she said to Raju as she fiddled around with her jacket, not sure whether to keep the buttons open or closed. She opted for the more casual open-buttoned look and just before she slammed the car door shut, Raju wished her luck, telling her he'd be back at the same spot at five thirty as he had an errand to run.

Bela made her way towards the entrance, keeping her head down as she felt a bit self-conscious. Apart from when she was filming, she was so used to being accompanied by Jaya, her family or her friends, that being alone for once felt quite odd.

At the main doorway she stopped so that she could peek in to see who was there before she went in. She had seen photographs of Om Shankara and was sure she would recognise him.

The reception area was directly in front of her and to her right was the hotel lobby. Bela had never actually been inside the hotel before but, just as she had expected, it was equally grand on the inside. It was tastefully kitted out with clusters of plush velvet sofas, armchairs and tables, and a small group of people were sitting towards the far end of the room by the huge winding staircase. Bela cautiously approached them before realising they were just a group of tourists.

Not quite sure where she was supposed to go next, Bela decided to venture out to the garden and have a look there. It was completely empty. '*Filmi* people, always late,' she mumbled, feeling slightly edgy.

Since it was only ten to five, Bela felt she should wait in the garden. A lot of people recognised her nowadays, and she didn't want anyone to see her hanging around on her own. Spotting a large double swing at one side of the garden, Bela opted to take a seat.

Twenty five minutes later, she was still waiting. There had been no sign of anyone and Bela was beginning to question whether this meeting was such a good idea after all. She popped back into the lobby area to look around again. There was nobody who resembled Om Shankara.

As it was now five fifteen and she was losing patience, Bela headed back to the reception desk to ask the receptionist whether she knew if any film-makers were in the hotel. The lady shook her head. She didn't appear to recognise Bela and judging by her miserable face that had 'I want to go home' written all over it, she probably didn't care.

Not knowing what to do and realising that Raju wouldn't even be back yet, Bela ventured back outside and once again sat down on the swing. She told herself that she'd wait for a total of fifteen minutes more, and if nobody showed up she'd head back home.

'I'm a top actress and my time is precious too, Mr Shankara!' she whispered, imagining what she'd say to the film director if he didn't apologise for being late.

Swinging away, Bela took her mobile phone out of her bag and put it on her lap in case somebody tried to call. Perhaps they were stuck somewhere, perhaps she was at the wrong hotel – there were several possibilities, she told herself. Ten more minutes passed but there was no Om Shankara and no phone call.

And then, suddenly, Bela got the distinct feeling that something odd was happening. She could hear a weird rustling sound coming from the big bushes behind her.

She stopped swinging, looked around, and the noise stopped. But as soon as she turned her back and started swinging again, she could hear the creepy sounds once more. Scared that it may be a fox or even a rat, Bela's heart began pounding. She pursed her lips tightly and proceeded to get off the swing as quietly as she could. She tip-toed over to the bushes, removed one of her high-heeled shoes – in case she had to defend herself against a wild animal – and pulled the shrubs apart.

'Aaaarghhhhh!' Bela shrieked.

It wasn't a fox or a rat. It was something much worse altogether. Crouched down on the floor, sniggering, pointing and laughing at her was Monica with two of her friends!

Bela recoiled from the mocking girls, stunned. She'd been set up! She started to run back towards the hotel, but lost her footing, slipped on the damp grass and ended up flat on her back while the girls laughed harder than ever.

Bela scrambled to her feet and tried to compose herself, but soon realised it wasn't even worth the effort – her pristine white jacket and designer white jeans were covered with mud and grass stains.

She felt awful. Not only had she been duped into coming all the way here under false pretences on a precious day off, she now looked a real state, too. As Bela hastily put her shoe back on, getting ready to flee the scene, she saw two young boys running into the garden from inside the hotel. They'd obviously seen her fall and wanted a closer look. They too were tittering.

No words came out of Bela's mouth and she just put her head down, hoping that, like the miserable hotel receptionist, the boys didn't recognise her. Monica and her sidekicks stalked past her, out of the garden and back into the hotel, still cackling loudly.

'Ha ha ha ha! That was the funniest thing ever, Mon,' said one of the girls to Monica.

'Definitely! She may be good, but she's not *that good*,' hissed the other one.

'And she's certainly not "the best" as she reckons,' added Monica, with real venom. 'Om Shankara signs Bela? Dream on!'

Chapter 7

'But I *did* think it was odd for them to send flowers and not contact me through Jaya,' Bela told Reuben, trying to explain why she had thought it was normal to be called to a casting meeting at such short notice. 'I *did* question why they didn't call me first.'

Bela had been sitting on her roof terrace, sunbathing in a stripy sundress and large square sunglasses, when the call from Reuben had come through. It was three days since the cruel incident at the Kohinoor Hotel, and although Bela was still mad at herself for falling for Monica's trick, the pain had begun to recede. Now, though, Reuben was making her feel worse than ever.

'Then why did you go?' he asked, quite angrily. 'Okay, so this was just Monica being a nasty little cow, but it could have been someone much more dangerous – crazy, even. You're a famous film star now. You can't just wander off on your own to an anonymous meeting. It's madness!'

'Mum knew I was going,' Bela said, hoping to convince him, and herself, that she hadn't been so foolish and impulsive after all.

'Yes, Bela, and that's a very good reason for you to have checked with someone else first. Mum's even more crazy and excitable than you are! When she gets an idea in her head, she doesn't think it through either – that's obviously where *you* get it from.'

Bela looked over at her mum, who was clearing away some clutter at the far corner of the roof garden. Deep down, she knew there was some truth in what Reuben said. 'But I thought it was Om Shankara,' she protested, still trying to defend herself, and feeling close to tears.

'So what?' came Reuben's sharp response. 'I don't care if you think it's Steven Spielberg. Next time, you DO NOT go off on your own. Understand?'

'Yes,' replied Bela, her voice trembling. Reuben was right – it could have been anyone. 'But you know what?' she said softly after a moment's pause. 'I don't get it.'

'What don't you get Bela?' asked Reuben, more sympathetically now.

'I just can't understand why anyone would want to plot such a nasty prank. I've gone over and over it in my mind and it's beyond me.'

'You're too nice, Bela, I keep telling you. Wise up, young girl – fast. I don't want to keep going on about it and after today, let's agree to not bring it up again. I just really hope you've learned a lesson or two.'

Bela felt the faintest glimmer of a smile appear on her lips. She was glad Reuben had got it out of his system and would now let the matter rest. She accepted that both she and her mum had been a bit naïve, but there was no point in dwelling on it. In fact, all she wanted to do was forget about the incident and forget about Monica. It was time to get out with the girls again.

* * *

At the end of the film shoot in Rajasthan, as the actors were making their way back to the airport for their connecting flight to Mumbai, Ajay Banerjee had given Bela an invitation to the soundtrack release of one of his forthcoming movies. At the time, she'd taken it and thanked him politely, but hadn't had any real intention of going along. As a busy star, Bela was invited to loads of functions but rarely attended them because she found it hard enough to make time for her own promotional events.

Now, though, she felt like letting her hair down and thought this might be the perfect opportunity. She liked Ajay, and thought it would be nice to catch up with him, but more importantly, Tara fancied the pants off him and Bela was certain she'd be up for it, even at such short notice.

First, she wanted to see if Priyanka could make it, and she punched her number into the mobile.

'Hiya,' Bela began chirpily, 'I really feel like painting the town red tonight, what do you say, party girl? It's been ages since we've all been out together – me, you and Tara. Probably not since our crazy school graduation ceremony.'

'Yeah, why not?' replied Priyanka, without a moment's hesitation. She loved going out and rarely needed coaxing. 'I was going to be reading up on skin cleansing techniques for my test on Thursday, but a night out sounds like much more fun. I'm game. Have you asked Tara?'

'I don't need to ask her,' said Bela with a smirk on her face. 'If I tell her there'll be a certain film star there, she'll be over like a shot. Just come to mine at about six o'clock and we can all get ready together. It'll be like the good ol' days!'

'Great,' said Priyanka, 'see you then.'

Bela then dialled Tara's mobile.

'Hi,' answered Tara, somewhat moodily.

'What's up, girl? You sound a bit down – as though you could do with some cheering up. How about a girlie night out tonight?' asked Bela, deliberately not telling her whose party it was. 'I know this great club in old Mumbai that has a members-only night tonight. And I can take anyone I like.'

'Normally I'd say yes – you know I would – but I'm really behind with my assignment,' came Tara's downbeat reply. 'I've got to finish it by the weekend or my course tutor will be really mad.'

'Loads of *filmi* sorts are gonna be there,' said Bela, enticingly.

'Yeah, but I really can't. I've got a lot to catch up on,' moaned Tara.

'It's the soundtrack release of Ajay's movie.' Bela played her trump card.

'I'll be at yours at six!'

'I knew that would work!' laughed Bela as she flipped her phone shut. Tara always made out she was behind with her studies, but she rarely was – her standards were just so high. When she wasn't being crazy she was usually studying, and Bela was sure one night out wouldn't affect her.

It wasn't even four o'clock and Bela decided there was enough time for her to dash across the road to her beautician for a relaxing facial and manicure.

Ninety minutes later, feeling thoroughly revitalised after the pampering session, Bela made her way back home. When she reached her house she was surprised to see that both her friends were already there, watching satellite TV and drinking lemonade from glass bottles in the living room.

'You're both nice and early,' commented Bela, looking a bit puzzled. 'Or am I late?' She glanced up at the clock and saw she was right – it wasn't six yet.

'Well, we don't have appointments for posh manicures and pedicures so we thought we'd come a bit earlier,' Tara told her. 'Plus we need to get the lowdown on who's coming to the party tonight. Is Marc gonna be there, too?'

'Tara! Make your mind up, girl,' said Bela, as she kicked her trainers off. 'I thought you were going for Ajay – it's Marc now, is it? And all those shopping trips you made with Ajay's mum – what a waste of time!' she laughed.

'I'm not fussy,' stated Tara, throwing a cheeky glance at Priyanka. 'I'll take either. Maybe Marc's mum will be a bit easier to please.'

All three girls burst out laughing. Bela felt really happy. She loved being with her friends and following all the unpleasant goings-on with Monica, she was more glad than ever that the three of them were still so close. Even though her own life had changed beyond recognition, Bela knew her friends weren't envious of her fame and fortune – they just wanted a slice of it.

It wasn't long before Tara and Priyanka were busily raiding Bela's exclusive wardrobe, looking for the latest designer garments to wear for the party. Bela showed them the bits and bobs she had set aside for them and they sifted through all the garments with glee. It was girlie heaven.

'Gosh, you lucky old cow,' said Tara, picking up a pair of Bela's gold-coloured skinny jeans and trying to work out if she could squeeze into them. 'No wonder Monica hates you – she probably had designer babygros but now it's you who gets sent all the bling,' she added, making a beeline for a glitzy black handbag. 'Can't you get me into the movies too?'

'Well, you've already got yourself noticed – who hasn't seen your online video clips? I reckon you may be in with a shot,' Bela said generously. 'If I can do it, you can too,' she encouraged, even though she didn't think Tara was cut out to be a lead heroine. 'I don't know about this dancing-around-the-trees lark, it doesn't seem to suit your personality, but comedy? Sure.'

'So what are we hanging around here for?' asked Tara. 'Let's get ready – get out there and mingle!'

Bela put on some 1980s disco tracks and the teenagers sang and danced around the room as they selected the winners from their shortlisted outfits. All three girls chose to wear mini denim skirts with plain-coloured tops: Bela opted for red, Priyanka chose blue and Tara plumped for a bright, look-at-me fuchsia pink.

Their look completed with vibrant eye-shadows and gold high heels, Bela was certain they looked as glam as any girlie pop band as they got into Raju's car to be taken to the Mumbai Mahal nightclub.

Once outside the club, Bela took charge and led her friends to a side entrance which had a flashing neon sign above the door that read: 'Private Guests Only'. She had a quick word with the doorman, who politely asked for Bela's autograph, and after she scribbled on his hand he waved them through.

'Gosh, he's never gonna wash that hand again,' laughed Tara, squeezing Bela's arm. She couldn't believe they could just walk into such an exclusive place.

Once they were inside, Bela looked around for Ajay. She saw him standing by the stage talking to two men, and she gave him a wave. He rushed over and they greeted each other with a kiss on the cheek and an embrace.

'Thanks for coming, Bela,' he said, with a huge smile. 'So nice of you to make the effort. I really hope *Jaan* is going to be a success.'

Bela hadn't even stopped to think about the name of the film they were here to champion, but she did a good job of pretending that she knew it all along. 'I hope so too. It sounds like an interesting movie,' she lied, with an equally broad smile.

Priyanka's eyes had nearly popped out of her head when the good-looking movie star made his way towards Bela. 'Is that Ajay Banerjee?' she whispered to Tara.

Tara shook her head. 'No, it's Michael Jackson. Of course it's him, stupid! I can't believe you don't recognise him. Maybe we should send you home for being so ignorant.'

Priyanka brushed aside Tara's sarcastic remark and just drooled, 'He is *soooo* hot! He looks a million times better than he does in the movies,' she said, barely able to contain herself. 'I was looking for Ajay at the awards function but I couldn't see him anywhere.'

After a slight pause, Priyanka turned to Tara and scoffed, 'And you were trying to get in there with his mum! As though she's gonna pick you as her daughter-in-law and he's gonna agree – deluded or what!'

'How do you know his mum doesn't like me?' shot back Tara, very defensively. 'And who's told you Ajay doesn't fancy me? We could be having a secret romance for all you know. Maybe we're already engaged… I don't tell you everything,' she snapped.

'Shhhh,' whispered Bela to her friends. 'Stop

bickering! You're worse than my parents, and that's saying something! It's embarrassing – we're supposed to be having fun, remember?'

Tara forced a smile, but she also folded her arms very tightly, and Bela knew she was annoyed that Priyanka had completely dismissed her chances with Ajay. Thankfully, before Tara could get into a full-pelt sulk, the lights dimmed, the music began to play and she very quickly reverted to her crazy old self again.

'Time to party! WHOO HOO!' she yelled, putting one hand on her hip and thrusting her other arm up, *a la* John Travolta in *Saturday Night Fever.*

Bela and Priyanka began giggling and slowly swaying to the beat of the music, but as they twirled about the dance floor Priyanka suddenly stopped. She strained her eyes as she tried to focus on something ahead of her.

'What's up?' asked Bela.

Priyanka pointed to the far end of the dance floor.

They hadn't noticed the huge publicity poster of *Jaan* when they'd come into the club because there had been a big group of people milling around at that end. But now, with the main lights dimmed down, the small fairy lights framing it meant it was hard to miss. Staring straight back at Bela and Priyanka were the faces of Ajay Banerjee and Monica!

'Uh-oh,' groaned Bela. If Monica was the heroine of *Jaan*, she was bound to be coming tonight. 'Ajay invited me to this launch party but I didn't think I'd come so I didn't even bother to find out the name of the film or who else was in it… Of all the places we could have gone.'

Tara finally noticed she was the only one shaking her bootie on the dance floor, and walked over to her friends. 'What's up, girls?' she asked. 'Looks like you've seen a ghost.'

'As good as,' sighed Bela, pointing to the poster.

'Oh no,' cried Tara, slapping her forehead in disbelief. 'After what she's done to you, we're here to celebrate her film! That's just great.'

'Ladies and Gentlemen,' boomed a strong, masculine voice over the speakers. 'Now we move to the main event of the evening: the launch of the soundtrack of *Jaan*. Please, put your hands together for the leading couple as we welcome the amazing Ajay Banerjee and the mesmerising Monica!'

Everyone in the club started clapping, including Bela. She had to be courteous for Ajay's sake. She looked around and could see there weren't more than sixty people present – it was a weekday and no-one had really heard of this movie. But the one person Bela definitely didn't want to see was just about to appear.

Monica walked in with four stunning girls, whose long, lithe bodies made Bela think they must be models. They made a beeline for the bar. Monica was wearing jeans and a sparkly blue bra-top that showed off the diamond adorning her belly button. She didn't seem to realise that she should be joining Ajay on stage and just carried on chattering to her friends.

A spokesperson from the record company releasing the soundtrack was standing on the stage next to Ajay. He was holding up a CD tied up in red ribbon and was supposed to be presenting it to the lead couple, but Monica was oblivious to this. She was now falling about laughing and wasn't going up on stage any time soon.

As Bela looked closer, she was surprised to see that Monica's mates were almost propping her up, although they also seemed to be having trouble standing upright. The giggles got louder and louder until the girls were almost crying with laughter.

'They're all drunk! Blind drunk! Even Monica. How funny,' Priyanka whispered to Bela.

Bela was shocked. Coming from a moderately conservative background where girls didn't commonly get drunk and disorderly, especially in public, she hadn't twigged what was going on. She knew that models were more open-minded about drinking and dating than the average Indian girl, but she didn't expect this kind of behaviour at such a formal occasion.

Ajay had also realised what was happening. He took over the microphone and tried to do a quick cover-up. 'Our leading lady, Monica, is so immersed in entertaining and talking to the public, she's forgotten to get on stage. Monica, please join us,' he beckoned.

'He's a good actor,' Bela chuckled to her friends. 'He must be squirming inside.'

'A hero in real life too,' drooled Tara. 'He's covering up for that ratbag, how sweet.'

Monica's friends started nudging her, and once she realised what was going on she took a few wobbly steps and clambered onto the stage to pose for photos. Ajay carried on smiling, showing real professionalism and not letting his annoyance at her show through.

The audience applauded and the spokesperson was finally able to present the CD. Ajay spoke into the microphone again, 'I'd like to thank everyone for attending tonight. Let's hope that the music of *Jaan* is appreciated because it is, in my opinion anyway, a melodious masterpiece. Thank you again and enjoy the rest of the evening.'

Priyanka realised that, at some point in the midst of Ajay's speech, Monica must have clocked Bela's presence. She was now staring at her in a rather aggressive manner. 'Look at her eyeballing you,' Priyanka said to Bela. 'She's definitely giving you dirties.'

'Nasty spoilt cow,' Tara piped up. 'God knows what her problem is, drunken tart! She hasn't seen me yet, imagine what she'd do if she found out I'm here – the VideoWeb impersonator!'

'Don't worry,' said Bela, trying to make light of it, but finding herself ever more repulsed by Monica. 'Ignore her. She won't say anything, she never does. She's a bully – a coward who just plots dirty tricks from a distance. Let's just enjoy ourselves. We're Ajay's guests, remember.'

Bela and the girls were just getting ready to boogie on down again, when Monica quite unexpectedly descended from the stage and strode towards the trio. 'Oh, look who it is,' shouted Monica as she approached them. 'It's the famous pop group, Girls Aloud. Or should I say Girls Not Allowed? I don't recall inviting you,' she said nastily, staring straight at Bela. She turned to Tara and Priyanka. 'And as for these two – *phuh*! Look what the cat dragged in!'

All around the group of girls, people had gone very quiet so they could hear what was being said. Two men, obviously reporters, were gleefully taking notes and a snapper stood ready to capture what he thought could become a sought-after photo. Monica's friends sidled up to her again.

'Well, for your information, we were invited by Ajay,' said Bela politely, but firmly. She would have loved to have it out with Monica for the nasty trap she had laid at the Kohinoor Hotel, but resisted. 'We're here to support him and I think you should do the same.'

'Why are you being so nice to her?' Tara said to Bela, frowning. 'She shouldn't talk to you like that – and we're not bits of rubbish that you dragged in, either. I ain't putting up with it. No way. She's right up herself!'

Monica's friends gasped.

'Excuse me,' said Monica, eyes narrowing and moving towards Tara in a threatening manner, one hand placed on her hip. 'Do I know you? I don't think I do. Well, I don't care who the hell you are, but I do know that this is *my* party and I don't like intruders.'

'Yeah, you tell 'em,' one of Monica's mates joined in, while the others all laughed. Tara was silenced momentarily. She was privately disappointed that Monica didn't recognise her from the VideoWeb clips. Tara had started thinking that she was a bit of a celeb in her own right.

Ajay, who had been busily signing autographs and talking to guests, was alerted to the scene that Monica was causing and rushed over.

Bela was glad to see him and raised her eyebrows as if to say 'not my fault, look at the state of her'.

'What's going on here?' Ajay asked, directing his gaze at Monica. 'These are my guests, is there a problem?'

'Guests? *Puh-lease!* You have no style, Ajay,' she answered bitchily.

At this point, Bela decided things had gone far enough. She was fed up of letting Monica get away with murder. She had been at the receiving end of too much already and Bela felt that Monica didn't deserve any more chances. Monica was being rude to her and her friends and she needed to be told.

'You need to get a grip on yourself, Monica,'

Bela began, completely aware that one of the reporters was now recording the confrontation on his mobile phone.

'Just because your parents were film stars once-upon-a-time, doesn't mean you decide who goes where. I've heard your "I was born here – she's an outsider" comments and, you know what? They're pathetic!' slammed Bela, really getting into her stride. 'Almost as pathetic as your stupid, childish pranks. At least I've worked to be where I am. Let's face it, you would never even have seen the inside of a film studio if it wasn't for your dad!'

Monica's face dropped. She was gobsmacked. She never thought Bela would have the nerve to produce such a verbal attack on her – and right where it hurt the most. Incensed, Monica took a deep breath in, stepped forward, and if it hadn't been for her alcohol-affected aim and Ajay's intervention, would have landed a firm, hard slap across Bela's face.

Ajay held Monica's wrist down for a good few seconds, only letting go when he thought it was safe. Monica's friends quickly dispersed.

'Truth hurts, does it?' said Tara, twisting the knife further, but also trying to impress Ajay. He was her number one hero all over again. Marc was out of the picture – for now, at least.

Monica ignored Tara's comment. She wasn't interested in what she thought – she was still furious with Bela. 'You make a few films that fluke it at the box office, win an award, and then you think you're better than everyone else and can go around dissing me,' snarled Monica, wildly. She took a deep breath in to try and calm herself down.

'Well, Miss Prim and Proper, I bet you'd like to know who's gonna be starring in Om Shankara's next movie, hey?' she said teasingly, bending her knees slightly so her face squared right up to Bela's.

'It's me and Marc.'

Chapter 8

'Come on Marc, stop chatting Bela up again – time to get back to work,' shouted Prem, *Mumbai Magic's* film director, as he busily framed a shot.

Marc, who had been filling Bela in about his plans to open up an acting and modelling academy in London, hollered back, 'Not my fault she's so beautiful, what's a man to do?'

He turned back to Bela and winked. Flattered, she giggled and then modestly lowered her gaze.

'Right, you two,' said Prem, moving over to position his lead pair. 'Enough of all this lovey-dovey business. Bela, face the camera and stand to Marc's left, like so,' he demonstrated, shifting her a few inches sideways, before going back to the camera to assess whether that had helped matters or not. 'Monica darling, you can stay where you are. You weren't really supposed to be sitting in the shot, but actually I think it works. In fact, you look fab like that – very moody.'

Peering over her shoulder, Bela thought Monica looked more miserable than moody.

Monica, who had been sitting sullenly on the sofa for ten minutes or so, gave a slight nod of the head to acknowledge that she had heard the director. She had skulked onto the set well after all the others this morning and definitely wasn't in the mood for conversation.

Bela felt she should be angry with Monica for her appalling behaviour the previous night. Now, though, looking at Monica's pathetic demeanour, Bela thought she deserved sympathy more than anything else. Being asked to leave the club for bad behaviour during her own film's soundtrack release must have been humiliating.

The release of *Jaan's* soundtrack had been celebrated with even more of a bang than anyone had wished, but now Bela wanted to concentrate on the job in hand and was determined to push all unpleasant memories of the night aside. She had to stay fully focused today. She had some quite emotional dialogues to deliver, and if she could do them justice this sequence could become a real highlight of the film.

The scene was quite a challenging one because Bela was required to portray a mixture of anger and upset. She had to accuse her on-screen lover, played by Marc, of cheating on her and then end the shot by breaking down in tears. Monica, playing the part of the other woman didn't have any dialogue to deliver; she just had to sit and look as though she was ashamed.

Concentrating hard, Bela stood next to Marc with a grave expression on her face while Prem made his final adjustments.

'What's up with our friend over there?' Marc whispered to Bela. 'She looks well upset.'

Bela was surprised that news of the nightclub altercation hadn't reached him yet, but she was certain it was just a matter of time. 'Wait until lunchtime,' replied Bela. 'I'm sure you'll have heard all about it by then.'

'Okay, stop talking you two,' the director cut in. 'We're ready to go… Lights, camera, action!'

'How can you say these things?' began Bela, looking pained. 'You lied to me. Not once, not twice...' Suddenly, she grabbed hold of Marc's shirt and pulled it so hard that a button popped off to reveal his smooth, muscular chest.

'You lied again and again and again! I trusted you, but you betrayed me. And for what?' she asked, the pitch of her voice getting higher with each sentence. 'For HER!'

She pointed at Monica, who was sitting with her face down and her hands clasped together in her lap. 'All for her! I thought she was my friend, but all that time she was trying to steal you from me. I hope both of you rot in hell!'

Bela broke down in tears and slumped to the floor in a ball, sobbing loudly.

'Cut!' yelled Prem.

It was a few seconds before Bela moved. She almost had to shake herself out of her role, she had got so immersed in it. Somehow, the pain and disappointment that her character was supposed to feel had become very real to Bela herself, and she was surprised to have produced genuine tears. All the anger and hurt of the recent days had just spilled out through the character.

'That was mind-blowing, Bela!' commended Prem, looking genuinely amazed. 'Gosh, for a little schoolgirl you sure know how to pack a punch.

I'm really impressed, well done.'

The unit members clapped, and Bela felt so pleased that she didn't even let the rather patronising 'little schoolgirl' comment bother her. But while everyone else was acclaiming her performance, it seemed that Monica was getting more and more wound up. As the compliments showered down on Bela, Monica frowned and folded her arms ever more tightly across her chest.

As soon as Prem announced it would be a while before the next scene was ready to shoot, Monica donned her huge, dark sunglasses, grabbed her bag and was off.

* * *

That night, Bela thought over the day's shoot. It had gone really well and made her keen to produce another praiseworthy performance the following day. But it was now almost midnight and Bela was battling with her lines. It wasn't that they were difficult to remember, she was simply trying to imagine how she'd behave if she were really being kidnapped. After all, it's not the kind of thing that happens every day, and she was trying to decide whether it would be more realistic if she acted hysterical, tearful or terrified.

'I prefer hysterical,' said her mum, who was watching with great interest. 'You wouldn't be crying if a dacoit called Jassa scooped you up and took you away, would you? You'd be screaming, '*Bachao!* Help! *Bachao!* Is anyone there? *Koi hai?*' she added, with dramatic effect.

Bela laughed. Her mum wasn't wrong – it's just that her approach was so over-the-top it was quite out of date for modern movies. 'Thanks for that, Mum, I'll bear it in mind,' she yawned, realising it was high time they both went to bed.

Having gone to sleep so late, Bela was running slightly behind schedule the next morning and arrived at the studio at nine, while most of the cast and crew had already been present for an hour.

It was a gorgeous day, with the Mumbai sun shining brightly and a very cool breeze blowing. Although Bela felt like taking it easy, she was acutely aware that shooting was due to begin at nine thirty and she didn't have a huge amount of time to play with. In fact, it was going to be a mad rush.

'Hurry up, Bela,' urged Prem, as she stepped out of Raju's car. He was hanging around in the studio car park having a cup of coffee. 'It's not like you to be late. Quickly, get changed and ready to shoot. Your hair and make-up people have been waiting for ages. I don't want any delays.'

Prem was widely regarded as a superb director. He had already made two very successful commercial films and was only 26 years old. He was also known for having a ferocious temper, and this made the people he worked with very nervous. Thankfully, Bela hadn't seen that side of him – she'd only heard about it.

'Sorry, Prem*ji*, I won't be long,' apologised Bela, quickening her pace. 'I'll be done by nine thirty, promise.'

Bela rushed past the film set towards her dressing room and noticed Monica, who was sitting in Prem's director's chair. Monica looked up at her and sniggered.

'How childish,' thought Bela. 'I'm late and she finds it funny.' She soon forgot about Monica, however, as she caught sight of Micky and Mili sitting close by. Bela signalled for them to come over to the make-up room and then rushed off ahead so she could put her outfit on before they got to work. The stylists ambled along behind and as usual, Mili was chatting away while Micky nodded politely.

Bela hurriedly opened the door of her dressing room and was just about to step in when she suddenly stopped. Micky and Mili, who were following behind, heard Bela let out an almighty scream. 'AAAAARRRRRRGGGHHH!'

She then slammed the door and ran, still shrieking, all the way back to the set.

Concerned, Micky dropped his make-up bag and ran after Bela, while Mili, who wasn't one for quick movements of any kind, just stood where she was with a puzzled look on her face.

When Micky reached the set, Bela was standing clutching her handbag tightly and shaking.

Crew members began gathering around her, eager to find out what had distressed her so much, and Marc, who'd just turned up on set, also dashed over to her.

'What's up, Bela, what happened?' asked Micky.

'R–r–r–r–rats! RATS... Hundreds of them... ev–ev–everywhere!'

'Rats?' repeated Marc. 'Where?'

Bela pointed in the direction of her dressing room.

'How the hell? Hang on–' remarked Micky. 'I'll go and have a look.'

Micky hurried back towards the make-up room, half-thinking that Bela must be imagining all this. He arrived at the door and put his hand on the handle. He paused. Micky decided he would open the door very slightly so he could peek in. Mili, waiting in the corridor, hung back and kept a safe distance.

As soon as Micky caught a glimpse of the inside of the room, he too slammed the door shut as fast as he could. Sure enough, as Bela had said, it was completely infested with rats. They were everywhere – on the dressing table, on the floor and scampering on the window sills.

'Yep, rats. Loads of the buggers,' he confirmed to Mili, who had a horrified look on her face. She ran all the way back to the set while Micky followed behind, chortling to himself. He had never seen the woman move so fast.

When they got back to the set again, Bela was being comforted by Marc, Prem and Bobby, the bit-part actor who was playing Jassa the *daku*. 'But I don't understand how they got there,' she said, looking perturbed.

'Maybe someone put them there,' suggested Marc.

'But who would want to put rats in my roo…?' Her voice tapered off. She suddenly remembered Monica's snickering laugh.

Bela looked over at Monica and everyone else

followed her gaze. Monica had her face buried deep in her dialogue sheet, trying to make out she was so immersed in what she was reading that she hadn't even heard Bela's piercing screams.

'MONNNNNNNNICAAAAAAAAAAAA!' yelled Prem, his face going so red that he looked as though he might well explode. 'Get your sorry backside here at once!'

'Huh? What's wrong?' she said, trying to look all doe-eyed and innocent. Behind her mask, though, Bela sensed that Monica was afraid, as though she realised her prank was about to backfire.

'YOU have gone one step too far, young lady!' yelled Prem. 'I take it you're responsible for this!' He looked very angry indeed and Bela realised that all those stories about his temper were obviously fact, not fiction. His eyes were wide open and he was almost shaking with rage.

'You've been gossiping about Bela, laughing at her behind her back and I've turned a blind eye to it because I thought you're young, and that you would grow out of it. But this is too much!' he shouted furiously.

'But–'

'Shut up!' screamed Prem. 'Save your breath. I don't want to hear it. I just can't believe that you put my whole day's shoot in jeopardy for the sake of your childish, petty squabbles! And after all the lengths we've gone to, to make sure you get the best scenes and songs! You're an ungrateful, selfish, spoilt brat!

'You know what?' he then added, somewhat less ferociously. 'I don't care whose daughter you are, the way I see it, you're trying to harm my movie and because of that, I don't think you deserve to be in it.'

'S–s–sorry?' stammered Monica. 'I – I – I don't know what you're talking about,' she muttered, looking close to tears. All around them, the cast and crew seemed to be holding their breath, too scared to make even the slightest sound in case Prem turned his wrath on them.

Bela made a decision. 'Oh, Prem*ji*, it can't be Monica,' she piped up. She had regained her composure and bravely took a few steps forward so she could speak to the irate director.

Everyone looked around at Bela, puzzled by this unexpected turn of events.

'I don't think Monica has anything to do with this,' Bela stated calmly.

'What are you talking about?' interrupted Micky, moving closer to Bela. While he wouldn't ordinarily involve himself in such matters, he felt he had to make an exception here. 'You know Monica's to blame.'

'No, she isn't.'

'Come on now, Bela. Prem has just admitted that she's been receiving favours – it's a travesty! he said, disgusted.

'I knew I could smell a rat,' said Mili, trying to make everyone laugh. But it was definitely a case of bad comic timing, and noticing some disapproving stares she went and hid behind a huge prop.

'No, this has nothing to do with Monica,' asserted Bela, glancing up at her make-up man. 'Monica was kind enough to send me congratulatory flowers the day after I won the Best Actress award. I know we've had a few communication problems, but we've sorted all that out,' she continued, using her very best acting skills to good effect.

'And,' she went on, now looking at Prem, 'Monica's recommended my name to a top director for his next movie, too. She definitely doesn't have anything to do with the rats. It's my fault. I've just remembered I stupidly left biscuits and fruit on my dressing table yesterday. Sorry, Prem*ji*, I'll call someone to get rid of them right away.'

Monica stayed where she was, too scared to move and feeling very confused by Bela's statement.

At one level she couldn't believe her luck, but she was still suspicious, and nervous that Bela would suddenly blurt out the true tale of what happened at the Kohinoor Hotel.

Marc looked over at Bela with a 'what-are-you-up-to?' look. Like Micky, he knew Monica was at the centre of all this, and had no idea why Bela was defending her.

'Okay, you lot,' said Prem, looking slightly less red. 'Stop gawping and get back to work. Bela, you come with me. Let's get you another room and get your hair and face done FAST!'

Prem still suspected that things weren't as simple as Bela claimed, but he decided it was a waste of time trying to find out what had really gone on.

'I don't care whose fault it is,' he growled at the onlookers. 'Everyone will have to stay here until we finish the shoot to make up for lost time. And if anything like this happens again,' he added, firing a glance at Monica, 'there'll be hell to pay.'

Needless to say, everything went swimmingly after that. Bela decided against her mum's advice of acting hysterical when Jassa Daku grabbed her from behind and dragged her away. She opted for a petrified look instead. Being a dream sequence, the kidnapping scene was so far-fetched it was hilarious.

Had it not been for the serious situation earlier, Bela was sure they would have had a whale of a time filming it.

Still, Bela was relieved to get the shot over with swiftly, and when pack-up was announced she couldn't get into her car fast enough. She jumped into the back seat with her costume and make-up still on, and it was only when Raju drove off that she began removing her heavy mascara and eye-shadow.

Once they had made their way out of the studio gates and on to the road, Raju, who had been given full details of the day's events by a floor assistant, asked, '*Didi*, why did you stick up for Monica? This isn't the first horrid stunt she's pulled on us and yet, just as she was about to get her comeuppance, you jumped in and saved her. I don't get it.'

Bela was very touched by his loyalty. It was nice to know she wasn't in this alone. But she also realised that he was genuinely bewildered, perhaps even upset by her actions.

'I don't know, Raju,' she explained. 'Prem was so angry... so vexed... Monica looked scared. It just felt like the right thing to do,' she added softly.

'But after everything that has happened between you two?' he asked.

'Well, I'm not proud of how I spoke to her in the club last night. I know she asked for it and I was provoked, but I was surprised at the things I said to her. It's not my style – it goes against my upbringing. Monica knows the real reason those flowers were sent to my house and how the rats got there. She has herself to answer to.'

Raju nodded slowly, impressed by Bela's kindness, especially when he remembered the state she was in when she left the Kohinoor Hotel.

'Well, that's very generous of you, but I can't be as forgiving. I just hope the brat's learned her lesson now, because her game's up,' Raju said, contentedly. 'And what about Prem admitting that Monica's been getting special treatment? That's not going to go down very well and it will be pretty embarrassing for them both. He's such a great filmmaker, I'm surprised he's been doing cheap favours like that. At least it's out in the open now, that's great.'

Feeling drained, Bela leaned back and looked out of the window, blankly watching the busy streets of Mumbai whizz by.

Strangely, she didn't think it was so great that Prem had admitted to helping Monica. Although his unwitting statement confirmed to Bela that she hadn't been sidelined in the song sequence because

BOLLYWOOD SERIES

Monica was better than her, it saddened her to know that this was allowed to happen in the world's biggest film industry.

Chapter 9

Although Bela's dad always told her that 'any publicity is good publicity', the story of Prem's 'confession' didn't help *Mumbai Magic* at all. It proved the film's script had been compromised to keep certain industry bigwigs happy, and people felt this cheapened the film.

It was also detrimental to Monica's image and

further confirmed in some people's minds that she was a spoilt rich kid who only got into the movies because of her father. It was for this reason that Monica's dad, Shashi Kumar, was furious.

'This is dreadful publicity for us,' he moaned to Dev Dhillon, the producer of *Mumbai Magic*, over the phone. 'All the papers have run with the story – it's bloody awful!'

'Tell me about it. I'm having to explain myself to everyone wherever I go,' said Dev.

'Well, my daughter has a big fan following and most importantly, she has a whole load of bloody hits to her credit,' Shashi Kumar went on. 'Her success is not just down to me, but thanks to that stupid, raging director you hired, people are beginning to think she's incapable of managing her own career. I want you to sort this problem out now. Turn it around, rectify it, do whatever it takes to undo the bad publicity.'

'But how?' asked Dev. 'The damage has been done. Prem, in a moment of madness, erupted, and I'm really sorry. But, Shashi*ji*, you have to admit that if Monica hadn't pulled that prank with the rats, we wouldn't even be in this situation. It's her own fault.'

'How dare you accuse Monica!' reprimanded

Shashi Kumar angrily. 'It had nothing to do with her. Bela admitted it was her fault. No, I don't care how you do it, but I want you to divert everyone's attention away from this bloody story or I won't loan you the money I promised.'

The phone went dead.

'Damn!' yelled Dev as he slammed the handset down in the office at his home. His wife, who had been listening at the door, realised this was not a good time to ask him if her mother could come to stay, and scurried off upstairs to bed.

Dev stayed downstairs until the early hours of the morning, smoking, making phone calls to various people and scratching his head. He had a mane of thick, black, curly hair, and each time he ran his fingers through it, the wiry mass got bigger and wilder. By the early hours, although he looked like a complete mess, he had come up with a master plan.

The only way to undo the bad press *Mumbai Magic* was receiving was by drowning it out with good publicity. And he thought the best way to do this was to host some kind of charitable event featuring the film's actors. It would have to be a glamorous, star-studded affair, and since the release of his movie was only a few weeks away, he decided that a pre-release fashion show and media party would do the trick.

'Yeah, I'm sorry I woke you up, but I've got it!' said Dev to Prem, explaining his plan over the telephone. It was still only six am.

'Think about it,' Dev continued, completely enthused by his own idea. 'Fashion shows are held in Mumbai all the time and they're all the bloody same – boring as hell. This thing will get people talking because we're not gonna use ordinary models – we'll get the film stars on the catwalk.'

'And how does the charity angle come into it?' probed Prem.

'Well, we can command a premium rate for the tickets because people will always pay top dollar for film stars,' Dev explained. 'But because we won't have to pay our models, we'll be able to donate a fair bit of money to charity and, I'm sure, keep a few rupees to ourselves.'

Both men laughed at the ingenuity of the plan.

'And how do you know the actors will do it for free?' asked Prem.

'Watch and learn,' he replied, with an air of supreme confidence. 'Come over to my place at ten, and I'll show you how it's done.'

As soon as Prem arrived at Dev's house, Dev

told his wife to make two cups of tea and cook up a traditional *paratha* breakfast for his guest. Then they got down to work. He dialled the number of the first actor on his list – Ajay Banerjee – while Prem watched intently.

'We're counting on you to attend,' said Dev. 'Everyone else has already said yes.'

After a moment's pause, Dev ended the call with a swift, 'Thanks, Ajay. I knew I could count on you.' He put the phone down and looked up at Prem, who had a wry smile on his face.

'I like your style, my friend – very sweet,' Prem acknowledged.

Both men shook hands and laughed heartily. Then, one by one, Dev called the key members of *Mumbai Magic's* star cast – from Marc to Deepa and Bobby, the bit-part actor playing Jassa Daku. They all agreed to take part.

Now there was just one person left to convince, and Dev knew she would be the hardest nut to crack – Bela.

A few days after being marginalised in the *Mumbai Magic* wedding song sequence, as she had vowed, Bela went to see Dev. She took Jaya along with her and they had both given him a really hard time. Dev had tried to convince Bela and Jaya that

Monica had been given the key performance in the song for the sake of the film, but neither woman believed him. Now, since Prem's outburst, Dev knew that Bela would see him as a liar. He wasn't in her good books right now, but he was going to give it a go all the same.

'I'm not sure it's a good idea,' Bela replied curtly. 'And my contract doesn't state I have to attend any pre-release fashion show. I only agreed to interviews and photo shoots. If you can't stick to your script, you can't expect favours from me.'

Bela wasn't usually as blunt or as rigid as this, but she wanted it to be known that she wasn't going to be pushed around any more.

'Hey, look, I'm sorry about all that stuff to do with the wedding song,' said Dev, putting on a friendly, casual tone, although he was feeling hot under the collar. 'But, you know how it is… Can't we let bygones be bygones, Bela, and work together for a good cause? You know this'll make a lot of money for the New Mumbai City Hospital. You'll be helping a lot of people.'

'Now that's just emotional blackmail – again,' snapped Bela. 'I can't speak now. I'll talk about it to my agent and get back to you.'

With that, Bela put the phone down and decided

to call Jaya straight away. She definitely wasn't going to ask her mum's opinion this time.

'I'm afraid you don't have a choice,' replied Jaya, without a moment's hesitation. She wasn't one to mince her words, which is why she had carved a nice niche for herself in the industry. Jaya managed three of the top stars in Bollywood and was regarded as a shrewd businesswoman.

'If you don't go, the headlines will scream: "Charity party snubbed by Bela". That will be even worse. You've got to go or we'll have even more bad publicity to contend with. You can definitely do without that.'

'Hmmm... I see what you're saying,' said Bela slowly. 'I'm not really happy about it though – it's one extra job for me and I'm already so busy… But I guess you're right. Damned if I do, and damned if I don't… I suppose it is for charity… Okay, decision made. Cinder-Bela shall go to the ball.'

Chapter 10

Dev's cunning plan seemed to be working. Over the next few days all the newspapers and entertainment magazines had articles dedicated to the charity fashion show. As Dev had predicted, the reporters had all picked up on the fact that the stars of the film would be modelling the clothes made by top designer Laila Khan.

'The event's getting some good publicity, Mum,' said Bela, as she flicked through the papers the evening before the fashion show. 'It's amazing that there's some good, positive coverage for a change. And it says here that not only will all proceeds from the ticket sales go towards the New Mumbai City Hospital's charity fund, but the garments will be auctioned at the end of the show, too, with money raised going to the children's ward. That's pretty good…'

'Yes, but who knows where the money really goes,' replied Bela's mum sceptically as she served up a delicious-looking rice dinner. 'You still trust these people?'

Bela could see her point. 'Well, we'll never know for sure, but I'd like to think I'm doing it for charity. Trust? Hmmm.' She pondered the question for a moment.

'You've never done a catwalk show like this before, have you?' asked her mum, as Bela hungrily eyed up the meal.

'Nope,' said Bela. 'Not like this, but I'm kind of looking forward to it now. It should be fun,' she added. 'Some of the older actors have never done any modelling at all, like Bobby, the guy who plays Jassa Daku, bless him. He said he's never even been to a fashion show before. It should be a good laugh, and hopefully we'll do okay and not make complete fools of ourselves.'

Bela was a little apprehensive. Although she had done a small amount of modelling for perfume adverts, they had all appeared on television and in magazines. She had no experience of catwalk modelling at all. This was partly because she was a touch short at just five feet and six inches, and also because she had never really had the chance, going from schoolgirl to superstar in the blink of an eye.

Monica, on the other hand, was an old friend of the ramp and had appeared in shows for all the top designers as well as commercials for all sorts of products from clothes to soap powder. Her striking looks – and her dad's contacts – had made sure that she'd got the very best jobs.

As Bela thought more and more about what the show would be like, her mood changed. She suddenly went very quiet and started pushing the food around her plate rather than eating it.

'What's wrong, Baby?' asked her mum, gently. 'There's something bothering you, isn't there? You having doubts about doing it?'

Bela heaved a deep sigh which seemed to come from the very pit of her stomach. 'Like I say, I just hope I don't make a fool of myself.'

'Of course you won't Bela. Why would you even think that?'

'Monica will be there again – and this is her territory. What if she pulls another stunt?' wondered Bela rather sadly. 'The last two pranks were pretty nasty, but this time there'll be loads more people there – celebrities, the press, even some politicians are supposed to be coming along. I'd hate to be at the centre of another humiliating scene, it'd be really awful.'

'Aah, you poor thing, come here,' said her mum, opening her arms out to give Bela a big, warm hug. She kissed Bela on the forehead, before adding firmly, 'Don't worry about that ratbag and don't you dare let her ruin your night, Bela. She won't do anything – your dad and I will be there to make sure of that. She's a coward and only ever attacks you when you've been on your own – just remember that. I'll look out for you, I promise.'

'You're right, Mum,' Bela nodded, feeling slightly more reassured. 'I'm sure Monica won't do anything, I was just being silly. I guess it's nerves about the show. Let's get some sleep. Night night.'

Bela gave Sheila a peck on the cheek and, trying hard to put the matter to the back of her mind, went up to bed. She was feeling more edgy than usual because there was one small detail she hadn't told her mum as it brought back so many unpleasant memories. The show was being held at the Kohinoor Hotel.

* * *

The day of the charity event was, as expected, pretty chaotic. Bela had to meet Sheetal, the choreographer, at midday so they could run through her steps. Although the fashion show segment of the whole event was quite short at just fifteen minutes, it would be the *pièce de résistance* of the night.

Not only were the actors doing the modelling, the background music score would be from the film's soundtrack too. The songs from *Mumbai Magic* were proving to be very popular even before the movie's release.

Bela had loads of missed calls on her mobile from Tara and Priyanka, no doubt wanting tickets and back-stage passes, but she was so busy rehearsing that she didn't even have time to call them back. Once Sheetal was satisfied that Bela understood what she would be doing, the actress dashed back home to get ready for the event.

At six pm, the street outside the Kohinoor Hotel was thronging with TV crews, photographers, journalists, members of the public with a ticket and also those with no ticket but just the hope of glimpsing one or two of their screen idols.

Bela stood on the red carpet outside the hotel along with Monica and Deepa, and they posed for photos together. All three girls looked dazzling in their Laila Khan dresses. The talented designer had carefully crafted three glamorous red outfits that were made from the same heavily-sequinned material but all with slightly different cuts. This made sure that no particular girl stood out, and the eye was naturally drawn to the shimmery effect of the girls together. Prem and Dev were delighted with the result.

'You all look gorgeous,' whispered Dev as he passed by the trio. 'But make an effort to smile, please. You're here because you want to be, right?'

Realising that the strain of having to smile alongside Monica was showing through, Bela made a bigger effort to show she was enjoying herself, as did Monica. Deepa, who didn't have any gripes with either of her co-stars, was the only one who was genuinely happy to be there. She just carried on beaming from ear to ear. Deepa was not as well-known as either Bela or Monica and she was lapping up the attention.

As Bela forced a wider smile and the flashbulbs popped, she caught a glimpse of Marc, who was also busily posing for the snappers along with Ajay Banerjee and Sanjay Suri. She thought all the heroes looked amazing with their slick black suits, red shirts and black ties, but Marc especially so.

Marc caught Bela looking at him and gave her a wink, before shouting out, 'Hey, girls, you all look great. Charlie's Angels watch out!'

All three girls burst out laughing. Thanks to Marc, there would be at least one or two genuinely happy snaps.

Dev, who was hanging around with Prem watching the photographers in action, was mighty pleased with himself for pulling off such a glittering event in record time. He was also relieved that the turnout was good and that he had garnered so much media interest. Shashi Kumar would surely calm down now and give him the promised money.

'Okay, that's the lot,' said a man dressed in a black suit and holding a walkie-talkie in his hand. He seemed to be the hotel's event manager and was telling the photographers their time was up and ushering the girls towards the large, dark double doors of the entrance.

'Stop herding us around like cattle,' snapped Monica. 'How about explaining to us where we're going and we'll make our own way there?'

The man stopped to look at her in a 'who-do-you-think-you-are?' kind of way, but decided against actually saying it. Instead, he responded, 'Madam, kindly head towards the entrance lobby, where security is waiting to escort you down to the Amber Room. Once you get there, you should wait for further instructions.'

Monica obviously didn't think this was necessary and wasn't about to wait for anyone. Without so much as a thank you, she broke away from Bela and Deepa and decided to make her own way.

Bela and Deepa did as they were told. They headed towards the building and then waited for security in the lobby area before going to the Amber Room to get ready.

While the stars busied themselves with their make-up and costumes, guests were invited to a glass of champagne in a room adjacent to the lobby. Then they proceeded to the main function hall and took their seats.

The visitors gasped in delight as they entered the grand-looking function hall. The walls were elaborately decorated with gold murals, and the whole room was flooded with soft, yellow lighting which gave it a calm but exclusive aura. The ceiling looked fabulous too. It was lit by thousands of tiny little twinkly lights, creating the effect of a beautiful, starry night.

Bela's parents rushed in just before the introductory speeches got underway. They had been delayed by her dad's game of golf, which had lasted longer than he had expected, and then by her mum, who had taken ages to get dressed. Nevertheless, peeking in to the hall, Bela was relieved to see they had turned up.

A spokesperson for the New Mumbai City Hospital opened the event with a poignant reminder of why everyone was gathered there.

'Or why they think they're gathered here,' thought Bela to herself as she listened intently to the speakers backstage. After what her mother had said, Bela now suspected this show had been put together just to save Dev's skin. Still, she reminded herself, she was doing it for charity so she needn't worry too much about it.

Fashion designer Laila Khan was up next. 'I'd just like to welcome you to the show and say a big thank you to the film stars who have given up their time to model for free, all for this magnificent cause,' she announced, and the audience clapped and cheered loudly to show their appreciation. 'I hope you enjoy the show and if you see anything you like, remember all the outfits will be auctioned off at the end of the night.'

As Laila Khan made her way to the long row of seats running alongside the catwalk, starters were served to the guests. As soon as they had polished them off, it was announced that there would be one live performance by a local singer, to be followed by the main attraction.

Unlike most fashion shows where models change their outfits several times, for this event the participants would only be modelling one costume each. Bela went to fetch her creation from Laila Khan's assistant, brushing past Monica as she did so. Both girls kept their heads down and swiftly moved on, and Bela couldn't help thinking it was strange how they'd been standing next to each other, smiling away for the cameras a few short moments ago, while in private, they wouldn't even look each other in the eye.

'Right, everyone,' shouted Sheetal, as she gave her models a last-minute pep talk. 'This is the first time such an event has happened here, so let's make it one to remember. Enjoy yourselves!'

Dressed in all their finery, everyone cheered and, with a mixture of excitement and anxiety, shuffled along to queue up backstage.

While most choreographers would save the best until last, Sheetal wanted to use Bela as the opening item to create a 'wow factor' for the show. Bela was quite pleased about this and was also relieved to know that she'd be able to get her job over and done with first.

Looking exquisite in a heavily embroidered, multi-coloured saree with bikini-style blouse and diamante-studded high heels, Bela waited anxiously behind the curtains for the music to begin and the cue to go on.

Monica and Deepa would be going on straight after Bela, and they stood ready and waiting just behind her. Bobby was to follow them, and then it would be time for the film's heroes to strut their stuff. Finally, the fashion show would end with the senior members of the film doing their bit.

Knowing Monica was so close behind made Bela feel more tense than she would normally be in these circumstances – she could almost feel Monica's icy presence at her back.

Then the music started to blare and the curtains began to move apart. Bela forced herself to relax by taking a deep breath and dropping her shoulders. 'Good luck, Bela,' whispered Deepa, patting her on the back.

Bela acknowledged the greeting, put her hand on her hip, broke out into a big broad smile, and propelled herself forward in as model-like a manner as she knew. All she had to do was walk to the front of the runway, do a couple of twirls, turn around, wave, and walk back. That was it.

Just as Sheetal had hoped, seeing one of the film's major attractions right at the beginning of the show really captured everyone's attention. Immediately, the guests stopped chattering to one another and looked at the stage.

Bela looked graceful and did a marvellous job of getting to the front of the ramp, but then she seemed to forget the script.

Just as she was about to turn, the bottom of her saree got caught under her heel. She struggled to free it, but lost her footing and toppled over, landing flat on her backside.

Once again at the Kohinoor Hotel, Bela wanted the ground to swallow her up. Being live on stage had always been Bela's biggest fear, and now her worst terrors were being realised.

This was worse than saying 'I love you' to Marc in front of all those people, worse than slipping on the grass, worse than the rather uncivilised nightclub argument with Monica, and even worse than the rats. It was like a really bad dream. Unfortunately for Bela, this was no nightmare. It was for real and she just wanted to cry.

She sat there for a few seconds, but it felt like an eternity. There were a few sniggers in the audience but for some reason, they seemed short-lived. Suddenly, the laughter stopped and the people began cheering again. They seemed to be looking at something behind her. Slowly, she looked up to see what was going on.

What she saw didn't seem to make sense. There was Monica, wobbling down the ramp with a comic expression on her face. A few seconds later, she landed flat on her backside right next to Bela.

The audience started clapping.

Monica then looked behind at Deepa, and very subtly pointed to the floor as if to say, 'you fall too'.

And so she did.

There was more applause.

Next, the three heroes of the film came dashing down the runway. Each one plucked his leading lady off the floor and paraded around with her before strutting back towards the curtain. As the couples disappeared behind it, the crowd began chanting 'Encore! Encore!'

It all appeared very romantic, and apart from the

actors themselves, nobody seemed to realise this was all being made up as it went along. Even Bela's parents thought this was how it was supposed to be – Bela's mum was clapping and whistling very loudly.

Backstage, Bela was still feeling dazed as Marc put her down again. All three heroes were laughing and slapping each other on the back, proud at how they'd managed to salvage the show from possible disaster. Only Bobby was a bit disappointed. The sudden turn of events meant he'd missed out on his part and he knew he was unlikely to get a catwalk modelling assignment again.

The senior actors had their runway routine to do now, and they set off as planned.

'You okay, Bela?' asked Marc, sensing that she must be feeling as though she'd let the side down.

'It's just so embarrassing,' she replied, looking down at the floor. 'I can't believe I fell.'

'Don't worry about it, these things happen,' said Marc sympathetically. 'In fact, I think you probably helped the show. I'd say that little performance was even better than Naomi Campbell's famous fall – you managed to fool the audience into thinking it was deliberate, which is more than she ever did. Clever girl!'

Bela managed to raise a slight smile. 'Well, if it hadn't been for Monica, everyone would have known it wasn't planned,' she admitted.

Bela peered over Marc's shoulder and saw Monica standing with Ajay and the rest of the gang. They were still congratulating each other for saving the show from being a complete fiasco. Bela caught Monica's eye and, without planning it, quietly mouthed 'thank you' to her. To Bela's complete surprise Monica walked directly over to her.

'It's okay, I owe you one,' Monica said sheepishly. Everyone around stopped chattering and strained hard to listen in.

'Sorry about what happened here last time,' added Monica, looking genuinely remorseful. 'I feel pretty stupid about it. I just got carried away by what people told me, and I started to believe everything I'd read about how you thought you were better than me, and so on. It was childish,' she continued, looking down. 'Anyway, thanks for sticking up for me in front of Prem – I thought I'd had it.'

'No problem,' said Bela, even more amazed by Monica's words than by her support on stage. 'I said some things to you in the nightclub that I shouldn't have, too. But I'm glad you realise that I never said all those things I was quoted as saying in the mags.'

'I'm sure you didn't, I'm sorry that I believed it all. Maybe I should have just checked with you first. I guess I was just mad,' admitted Monica.

'It's okay,' replied Bela, looking around at all the people who were watching this unbelievable scene. 'I think it's best if we just forget about what's happened in the past.'

'Sounds like a great idea to me, I'm happy to do that,' nodded Monica.

'Well,' said Bela. 'Why don't we all just have some fun for a change – starting with now…'

Monica broke out into a big broad smile. 'That's a great idea!' she enthused, and her eyes twinkled mischievously. 'And I know exactly how to make this an evening to remember.'

'Hey, Monica, hold on,' interrupted Marc, 'If this involves rats or the like, tell me now as I'm out of here!'

Everyone laughed.

Monica whispered something to Bela, who in turn whispered to Deepa.

Bela then linked arms with Monica on her left and Deepa on her right, and they all giggled as they made their way back into the main hall. As the starlets appeared through the double doors, the snappers all clambered over each other. They all wanted to capture the mood and the moment, knowing that this genuinely happy sight would make a very rare shot indeed.

Your thoughts...

'It is a great book, something different', **Anisha, 11**

'Now I know what it feels like to be a Bollywood actress!', **Tina, 12**

'An inspiring story telling us to never give up, even when people rival against us', **Nadja, 14**

'A book based on Bollywood stars is amazing. I can't wait for the next one', **Nashrah, 13**

'I loved it. Seeing the photos of the actresses and their outfits made it even better', **Jane, 12**

'It was like a real-life dilemma', **Nish, 14**

www.BollywoodSeries.com

Book order form

You can order further copies of this book direct from
Famous Books with FREE UK DELIVERY.

To order further copies of *Bollywood Series: Starlet Rivalry*,
please send a copy of the form below to:

Famous Books
Orders Department
2 St Peters Rd
Southall
Middx UB1 2TL

Alternatively, visit www.bollywoodseries.com and
click on the 'Buy Me' link to order online and have
the book delivered direct to your door.

Please send me _____ copies of *Starlet Rivalry*.

I enclose a UK bank cheque or postal order, payable to
Famous Books for _____ (at £5.99 per copy).

NAME
ADDRESS

POSTCODE
EMAIL

Please allow 14 days for delivery. Do not send cash. Offer subject to
availability. Please tick box if you do not wish to receive further
information from Famous Books ❏